T0107399

COVER of DARKNESS

COVER of DARKNESS

DAN BEL-TEMPO

iUniverse

Cover of Darkness

This is a work of fiction. All of the characters, names, incidents, organizations, and dialogue in this novel are either the products of the author's imagination or are used fictitiously.

iUniverse books may be ordered through booksellers or by contacting:

iUniverse
1663 Liberty Drive
Bloomington, IN 47403
www.iuniverse.com
1-800-Authors (1-800-288-4677)

ISBN: 978-1-4917-6000-0 (sc)
ISBN: 978-1-4917-5999-8 (e)

Library of Congress Control Number: 2015903236

Print information available on the last page.

iUniverse rev. date: 02/25/2016

This novel has three themes: United States Marines Corps Lieutenant Cooper is in command of a special detachment.

A Fallen Special Agent of the Federal Bureau of Investigation, Bruce Prescott, is politically incorrect by not informing the local police about several narcotic raids he is contemplating.

Josh, who returned home and is the older brother of Rachel, a naval officer in command of a very huge organization of recruiters and is definitely eye candy. Brother Josh creates a fabulous 15-piece orchestra and is ready to make some great money and in doing so meets a great diva that wants him.

Recognition of Kari Vanderweit for her contribution in miscellaneous activity.

In an underground hideaway reflecting a one-lane road several U.S. Marines are having a great reward eating lamb, steak, chicken and roasts, as they are drinking 3.5 beer and diluted wine. They cannot be heard as this hideout was made soundproof by the Navy Seabees, a construction battalion, giving these troops a very safe place to be in just before returning to their ship. One Marine says, "I don't know what happened to me, but I felt extremely well trained because the scum of the earth were taken by surprise and that surprise said it all.

"The surprised look on their faces was so rewarding: The disbelief in their face that they would be dead in seconds with a terrified expression. There is nothing like razor sharpness. I was extremely fortunate because I got to kill three of them all the same way.

"I'm an ace actor. Some of them even liked me as I created curiosity and delivered death."

PREFACE

A graduate of Annapolis Naval Academy that had been intimidated by a lieutenant to buy Marijuana from him and became a victim of exposure and was disgraced becomes a member of the U.S. Marine Corps. His attitude was to do all in his being to be the best of the lieutenants in his company. His attitude brought him promotions before any other Marine had made. He became a company commander with the rank of Captain, being way ahead of his peers. His detachment masters the art of aggressiveness to look, speak and act like insurgents and when the opportunity arose to take their life via a knife, dagger or cutting wire placed around the insurgent's throat.

Chapter

One

Rachel was a favorite of her commanding officer at Annapolis Naval Academy and he managed a promotion for her to command recruiters in the New York metropolitan area to reach colleges, universities and high school seniors for the Navy and Marine corps. She is in the throes of getting herself settled in, as she is a nervous wreck in dealing with something totally new to her. She is putting her belongings away and extremely worn out as she goes about what she is doing. She is talking to herself and is at the threshold of becoming loud. "Rachel! Shut up and get yourself squared away." She goes into the conference room and switches on the lights. Three panels of fluorescent light go popping on. "What a large table it has, with offset lights. It's beautiful in here. I really like it very much."

Finally she feels like she's getting somewhere. There is a knock on the door and she is leery about it because the super is a lech. He comes across as being nice, but still a lech.

"His eyes didn't miss a thing as he undressed me." Now the door bell went. "I'll bet he wants to pretend he forgot to tell me something. Well, I'm not going to find out standing here." She walks to the door and looks through a spy hole. "It's a guy but not him. I can't see him that well."

CHAPTER
TWO

"Commander! What are you doing here? You're supposed to be on that carrier."

"Thanks so much, Rachel, for advising me on where I should be. I have a lot of explaining to do. Well, do I come in or tell you everything at the door?"

"What's there to tell?" she asks. He seemed to be falling apart. He wanted so much to hold her.

"Well, for one, I'm not a commander. I am an FBI agent and was on a sting when I met you at the Academy." He advises he was on a mission.

"I heard something about a sting; you were behind that?" She looked shocked as she asked him.

"Yes, I was behind that. Rachel, you have no idea how much I have missed you. I didn't go to a carrier. I went to another under cover assignment, at West Point for the same thing. A sting on drugs, namely Marijuana."

"I'm having a hard time digesting this. So all that romance was a big front for you?" She was totally set back.

"That was the only thing I did that was not phony. I cannot get you out of my mind. That's why I'm here. I want to get engaged to you."

"Whoever you are I don't know you; perhaps you'd better make yourself more defined."

"I posed as a naval officer. My name is Bruce Prescott and like I said, I'm with the FBI. Does that help?"

"It's good for a starter and you can buy lunch for me! I'm giving you a break; that you can be thankful for."

CHAPTER
THREE

"I'll tell you what," said Bruce. "We'll have a quick lunch of sandwiches and on Sunday I'll take you to dinner at a high class restaurant, with a romantic blend. Would you do that for me?" Rachel looked at him sort of like she had suspicions about him. "Rachel, don't look at me that way. Let's say I fell in love with you while undercover. Please, give me the opportunity to enjoy being with you. It's a real need I have."

"Well, I'll admit I had strong feelings for you at Annapolis. Although I hate to say it, you are a very handsome guy, standing at what, six feet two inches? O.k. we'll go high class on Sunday if you will get so much joy out of it." Bruce's face showed great elation. He was all smiles and felt wonderful. As he was departing he thought to himself, *She is so gorgeous. What beautiful children we would make. My heart is pounding so hard there is a chance I could crash this car.*

This looking like a fox was troubling to Rachel; she would quickly settle for being just pretty. She had inherited an all-male staff of recruiters. *They're going to undress me whether I'm their boss or not. Well, it's better than being homely looking. What I have to do is make them afraid of me to a degree. I'll see how that works. I'm beginning to wish I was back at Annapolis.*

Chapter
Four

The sandwiches were delicious. Rachel enjoyed a Tuna Salad and Bruce a dripping hot roast beef sandwich. "Mmm, this Roast Beef is so good I'm tempted to get another one." He didn't realize he had just a bit dripping from the corner of his mouth. She laughed at it. "Is something funny?" he asked.

"No," she answered. She thought he looked cute with the drip. "They gave you a lot of meat. Roast beef is no good for your veins; don't you know that?"

"That is being overridden by my taste buds. I'll have apple pie alamode for dessert. What's the name of this place, anyway?" asked Bruce with an inquiring look on his face.

"Sherman's Catering. They have a caption that says 'where you just cannot get enough.'"

"Do you have a parking space for your own car? It doesn't look like you would have a problem."

"You're right! There is no problem. I like my official car. It's the new Ford Taurus. I'll tell you one thing I don't like, though. The super is a nice guy, but I can tell what's on his mind when I have a conversation with him."

"It's your fault, Rachel! Sometimes I don't think you realize how gorgeous you are. You are eye candy to the male eye. What are you going to do in your new position?"

"Be a bad-ass boss. I have to. I have to make my subordinates be afraid of me so that they don't concentrate on my being what you call 'A Fox'. I have surprise visits on the top of my list. You don't realize it but my authority goes quite well up the East & Hudson Rivers."

"My spread is even larger than yours. Narcotics is to the extreme. I'm going to ask for more agents. There are so many dealers, known as cells. They have firearms they think of as toys. Gee, they look and feel so nice. What they need is their own firing range so that they don't just shoot each other just for the fun of using their deadly toy."

"Thinking back to Annapolis, I can't get it out of my mind how effective you were as my pretentious boss."

"What's the sense in doing uncover work if one is not convincing? What I didn't expect was to find a subordinate that was going to blow me away. Some women just don't realize how attractive they are. Above everything that I do going forward is to get that gold band around your finger. You just don't realize how badly I have it for you. I need to be engaged to you in the next few months or it will drive me insane. I don't want anyone else to have you."

"Well, don't figure on attempting to hide me from the public. O.k. Thank you for lunch and I'll see you Sunday evening for a lovely, as you said, romantic dinner."

She gave me a peck on the cheek and was gone.

CHAPTER
FIVE

I had just come from a meeting and was going to my office when I saw what looked like my possible boss coming from the other way. A strapping, handsome man appearing to be a Navy commander, he sort of slowed down when he saw me and curiously asked if I was lieutenant so and so. When I gave him an affirmative he explained he was taking the former officer's place. This made him my boss and also provoked my feelings about working for him. He was just too handsome for me to work with him. He, on the other hand, was smiling brilliantly, like he had won a new car or something, like he had struck it rich. He advised he had just come from the captain's office and when he found my office to be empty he sort of thought I was his new subordinate. We talked right in the hallway for quite some time. I showed him to his office and we spoke of the petty officers under his command.

That seems like light years away. Despite Navy regulations, we found a way to get around them. We had a bit of a romance, starting with the yearly dance as chaperones. He never did behave like a Navy officer should to some degree. I use to have to remind him that he was not acting Navy. It was really fun. He was very humorous.

Well, that was then and this is now. She started to look into her organization and prepare for a conference with her staff. She had fifty recruiters under her, including female petty officers and Marines. They were about 12% of her staff. She thought they would all be men until she checked out the roster. However, she knew in her heart of hearts she was still going to be the FOX.

CHAPTER
SIX

She had her eye on the Midtown recruiting office in Times Square. She watched the goings and comings. They were not paying any attention to her as she was approaching. She was making a surprise visit. They were in a lull and were over-relaxed. There was a gunnery sergeant and a staff sergeant. They were paying no attention to her. They were in their own world making jokes. This told her they were not even paying attention to potential recruits. She let it slide for another minute. She then reentered the office and it was the same. She then walked straight up to the Gunny while he had his head down. He told her to take a seat until he was ready for her. However, the other recruiter jumped up and yelled, "OFFICER ON DECK."

He looked up in shock and saw Rachel standing over him. He shot up and stood at attention. She gave the big guy a staring down. He just stood frozen at attention. She said nothing while he was trembling. She felt great; he must be shitting his pants. She walked around between their desks and looked at the both of them.

"Somehow I have the feeling the U.S. Marine Corps would not consider each of you for a promotion. I mean, you guys were having fun on Navy time, weren't you? There is nothing like seeing the troops when they're not expecting you, isn't that right, Gunny?"

"Yes ma'am," said the Gunny as he came close to fainting.

"Yes ma'am does not cut it with me, Gunny! You'll address me as commander. Is that understood?"

"Yes, commander."

"Do you understand that, staff sergeant?' she barked. with the greatest of irritation on her face.

"Yes, commander."

"I'm very disappointed in this visit to your office. If I ever catch you so relaxed at a future time I will take a stripe away from each of you, depending on the circumstances. You knew there was a new commanding officer at this point. Why show your worst when you could have shown your best?" Despite the chewing out she felt bad for the recruiters. Well, it had to be done.

Chapter

Seven

As Bruce's' group awaits him in the conference room, they're not happy when these meetings come up. One agent places his head on the table, not caring if he looks very unprofessional. Others are looking out the window like it's an escape hatch. There is thumping on the table. Among the personnel, there are two women that are special agents. They are among the first women that became agents. They are semi-lookers (meaning that they're attractive, but not outstandingly so).

The room has a reputation among the agents as the bad news room. They're waiting on Bruce. There, on the wall, is the photo of the Director. Another frame work is a short history of the bureau, and it takes up after Hoover had left, like it was a new start after he left and they appreciated his leaving. As Bruce entered the room and looked around he made a loud statement. "Why do I see a lack of professionalism?" He takes his seat at the head of the table with a smile on his face. "Why is it that you professionals aren't looking like what you're supposed to be? Oh yes, they don't know what's coming up; only that they know they won't like it. Well, I was there just as you are. I was assigned undercover work at our service universities. I had a boss that didn't like me. I gave him no reason to feel that way, either. It was just the luck of the draw for me."

He passes out a document and it circulates the table. There are question marks on their faces. "What is this all about?" said one of his storm troopers.

"You haven't been privy to this yet. We have an agent up the East River and another high up on the Hudson. They have advised me of drug movements to distributors, both large and small. They have pinpointed these groups. These agents are the cream of the crop in what they do. I'm extremely proud of them."

He rose and did a little bit of walking and then he pulled down a chart. This chart focused on the Hudson and East River valleys. He took a pointer and showed where the activities were on both rivers. "I'm asking for reinforcements for several raids. It's too big for just the lot at this table. Special Agent Scarponi will be taking charge for the farthest northern spot on the higher Hudson; Special Agent Rainwater will do the most northern point on the East River."

These agents were the females who served with an outstanding reputation for getting things done the right way. Other agents were glad to work with them, and then, some of our troops should not have been there.

CHAPTER
EIGHT

Recruiters were starting to fill the conference room. Rachel had the door open and directed them to it. They were acknowledging each other and asking how each other's numbers were. News was coming that their numbers were finally showing some promise.

"Gentleman, please be seated. It is only lately that some progress has shown up in the numbers. There is going to be a major campaign to bolster our numbers. I'm bringing in a candidate for approaching NYU, Columbia and other state schools.

"This candidate needs to be the best of the best. I have applications coming in from both forces and will choose only three of them, and then one of the three," she explained.

They liked what they heard and were showing a bit of excitement. "Are there any questions?" Rachel asked.

"Are we going to work with this candidate?" someone asked.

"Sure, you'll be backing him up with applications.

You'll accompany him/her to the schools they go to."

As she spoke she could feel the vibes of some of the men.

They watched her every move she made. Then she started to become a little annoyed, but what could she do? She had great treats for them and provided everything she thought they could appreciate. She even threw in some cookies she baked herself.

But she didn't want them to know she had baked them. She catered in sandwiches, several hoagies, Éclairs, cream pie, and small pizzas.

Chapter
Nine

I met her at West Point cafeteria where the officers sat in the chow hall. She looked at me and gave me a great big smile. So I said to myself, Lookie here. *She had, of course, never seen me before and was actually flirting with me. Here I carried a major's rank and she was a superior officer. She was a lieutenant colonel, around the corner from being a full colonel. After about two months, she was actually pushing me to go out with her for dinner. Well, we have to get to know the people, and I was on the FBI's credit card from here on. We had a great time and she took my head, brought it to her lips and gave me a very sensuous kiss. I thought I would be able to use her until I started suspecting her. Then I actually saw her meeting a student on a staircase and within five seconds I witnessed an exchange of money for Marijuana. I was crushed and went into a tantrum; Bruce, of course went to the privacy of my room. In a way, I was brokenhearted. I liked her a lot. I sicced the NCIS on her. Thinking back on how much she wanted me, this is no way to make a living. After checking closer into her background, I saw that she was related to general officer. It was her uncle that started the drug chain because he didn't get a promotion to a fourth star. Well, she fell right in line with him. What a waste of a gorgeous woman; she was worse than a prostitute. The general made connections in Afghanistan. Who would suspect some one of his stature to be a major distributor? No, he wasn't a distributor in the sense that others are. His destruction of human life was like one entity as big as a bank.*

"However, you're not doing the undercover work; you're making the raids and arrests. Half of the personnel at this table have already made several raids. We have about 10 virgins here.

"Mike, take the lower Hudson and Steve, take the lower East river. We're going to come down on them tomorrow night like a hammer.

"They have been operating in plain sight. They have been putting their coke in a wholesale milk tankard. When they made deliveries, they sucked it out of camouflaged back portals. The garage appears to be a milk delivery system. What creativity; it gives me pause to wonder if they're laughing at us all the way to the bank.

"When will the population of this country stop making a market for these brazen killers? I understand out in Afghanistan their poppies are a supply for the Taliban and some of our own money is getting to them down in the most remote parts in the hills. Well that's neither here nor there. Our problem is in the South."

Chapter

Ten

News had gotten out about the campaign and candidates were being fielded from companies in Kuwait. There will be a complimentary celebration for the candidates company. This was a really big deal for these companies. It was the talk of the Mid-East. The winner would be in the "Navy Times." It would make it easier to get a promotion when you were eligible to be a lieutenant commander and you separated yourself from the others.

"Third brigade, 2nd Marine division, 5th Marines, Charlie company. I think I have just the lieutenant you're looking for colonel. His name is Conrad Cooper. He is my most outstanding platoon leader. I sent him to advanced training a few months ago. You say the candidates are going to be from around the world. To be honest, that seems to me like a bit of doing. That's also a lot of money out of the Marine Corps budget. The candidates are going to report to a commander in the New York City area. Do you want me to send Conrad up for you to meet him? You'll come down and we'll take him to lunch at the officer's club. I'll call him in." Conrad Cooper was going to join Rachel for consideration for this special assignment, if he passed muster.

Lt. Conrad Cooper was one of three to five Marines to get to be interviewed by Rachel. She had to test the mettle of this candidate. She decided to attempt to distract him by crossing her legs a bit. She was hoping one of them would be consumed by the importance of her work. Considering he was coming from somewhere where he there was a shortage of the female population, she did not want another master sergeant situation. *You have some nerve Rachel. You're looking for a man made of iron. Don't you feel you're being unfair? My goodness, you may land up with no chosen rep for your campaign. It will serve you right. One look at your legs and it's all over but the shouting. Should I or shouldn't I? It has to be done,* she thought to herself.

She looked at her candidates and was awed by the fact they were all handsome officers. *Drat it. They would be. Bruce is going to have a field day when he finds out. What busting material I'm giving him. Well, he doesn't have to know that! Unless I slip up, well, they're all handsome; however, not as handsome as Bruce,* her mind kept saying.

"Attention candidates." She looked around. Their eyes were on her while they held their breath. "I'll be done with the interviews tomorrow because I had too many calls from superiors. As much as I would like to give you a treat to the city's entertainment throughout the evening, it's just not in the budget. In fact, I should have taken fewer candidates, from one battalion. However, I promise you will eat well and I have some entertainment available right here. You are free to sightsee New York if you wish. Just don't bring any ladies back with you. Goodness knows you'd have no trouble getting female attention.

"I'm going to start with Lieutenant Rydell; if you would follow me into the conference room."

"Yes Commander."

They walked into the long polished looking room. It was a bit nerve-racking because it was so official looking. He thought to himself, *This room can hold forty people. Some suite the commander has.* They both sat down. She sat at the corner of the table so that she could pull her little stunt. He sat at the table edge. She even had the audacity to wear a tantalizing perfume. If all of them flunked her test it would serve her right. She was setting them up for failure.

"This is one of the most important campaigns there ever was because we no longer draft troops."

Then she became naughty and watched him. However, he was looking straight at her. *Wonderful, absolutely wonderful.* "You'd be very hard at work trying to convince students to enlist. I can't advise you on how to approach it but you have to deal with the personalities before you. Two recruiters will be at your sides to aid you in any way you may want them to. While you're doing this you're their commanding officer. It's a lot of responsibility. Do you think you're ready to handle it?"

"I won't have a problem, Commander."

Late the next day she had finished and to her surprise no one took the bait. This also made the process difficult. She went through their records again. Conrad Cooper had been at Annapolis when she was there at the same time Bruce was there. He did not graduate with his class. She called him in for a run down.

"Lieutenant Cooper, your record shows that you had trouble at Annapolis. Would you care to clear that up for me?"

"Commander, the person truly responsible for that was the lieutenant that was murdered, if you can recall that. He intimidated me and several other midshipmen into smoking marijuana so that he could enrich himself. I was going to have words with him about the illegality of it all by not going back to him and if he persisted, then I was going to go to the commander of troops. During that time of thought he was murdered and that was the end of that. However, NCIS called on me and grilled me mercilessly and stripped down my auto. I finally caved in and confessed my buddies up as well."

Chapter
Eleven

"We had a new arrangement with the commandant because of the situation. I was the only one of the three of us to be able to graduate, however, not with the class. I'm here today because I made myself make up for what had happened and decided to go into the Marines and be the best that I could be. Fortunately, my commanding officer took note and sent me for training the other officers did not get. When your announcement arrived the Battalion commander told my company commander he wanted a man and I was the man that my C.O. told him about. I've given the corps my very best. I'm told I'm the best of all the platoon leaders; of course, sir, you realize that is no easy feat. When you get that kind of attention others are not as happy as you are."

"Now that you have brought me up to speed on your background I'm going to make a gamble on you and have you do the campaign. Please don't let me down, Lieutenant."

"Not a chance, Commander. I'll get us more troops. How long do I have?"

"About two months. I can't afford any more than that. In fact, I can't even afford that; but we will make do with it."

Chapter

Twelve

"Charlie 10 to Osage 1, we are here at north east river. It is quiet. There does not seem to be any one around. Waiting for orders, Osage 1."

"Osage 1 to south Hudson 1, what activity is going on?"

"Hudson 1 to Osage 1, we are going in. We're about ready to bust in the door. Four agents are at the door and two agents are in the back. I'm giving the order now to bust in. Are you ready?"

"Agents to Hudson 1, we are ready. That's a go!!"

As soon as the door was broken into the agents flashed in and told everyone inside to freeze. However, one of them raced to the stair and ran up. He got up on the roof. He set up a block for the door he had prepared. He sprinted right to the end of the roof and took a suicide dive. One of the agents from the back held back from entering and saw the guy in flight and heard him land with a big thud. Instead of entering the back he went to the one that jumped and looked at him. His eyes were open and blood was running out of his mouth. The agent felt for a pulse, knowing there would be none, but checked anyhow. Not a beat to be had. "Agent Dowd to Hudson 1."

"Go ahead, Agent Dowd!"

"Hudson 1, we have a suicide here."

"Agent Dowd, he is only one casualty. Three of them have been fatally shot and we have four prisoners. I'm on my way."

Hudson 1 circulated among his team of agents and was looking the situation over. He moved his head up and down to register all that he saw.

To no one in particular he said, "Call for a paddy wagon from the NYPD and medical people, along with the Coroner's office."

"What a waste--four distributors we cannot question. Let's hope we can get some info on these three.

"Hudson 1 to Osage 1."
"Go ahead, Hudson 1."
"Osage 1, we have three for questioning and four are dead."

"Hudson 1, leave your men to finish up and report in. We also seem to have three dead and ten to question for the other raids. We did well tonight! I believe we can learn a great deal from all the lowlifes. We've called into the NYPD for all kinds of help. You know something; I don't think they appreciate us. We're going to have a hornets' nest in the next couple of days. They don't mind helping, but we had too big of an operation. Regional special agent, here we come."

Chapter

Thirteen

"So, you had some night, eh," Rachel stated while lunching with Bruce.

"The NYPD is slightly miffed at us. I hadn't notified them of what was going down.

"I was wrong; I should have. Maybe it's because they don't like us. We're the big wheels of law enforcement and they say we have big heads."

"Do you think there is something to that, Bruce?"

"What! Us having big heads?"

"Yes, you guys having big heads," said Rachel.

"We do occasionally act like that. I'll admit to it. We can't help it if we're smarter than they are," he said smugly.

"Well, excuse me Mr. Federal man."

"Not you too, Rachel?"

"No, not me too," Rachel answered.

"How are things going on your side of the fence?" Bruce inquired.

"Well, I've got my representative from the Marine Corps. He got into trouble about the time you were at Annapolis. Do you know anything about that?"

"Sorry, I cannot speak of any assignments I had. Strictly classified."

"Well, he said he was visited by the NCIS and questioned at length. His car was torn apart and he threatened to sue. The agents told him to sue. See where it gets you. Well, he told me how it all happened and how he has tried to make up for it. Seems he has made up for it and is in great standing with his superior officers. I also like the guy. He almost made me feel like fixing him up with one of my recruiters. Who knows, if things turn out well; I just might do that."

"When is he starting?"

"He already has. He went upstate this morning at the very edge of my territory. He's at Kingston University."

Chapter

Fourteen

"Sir," one of his recruiters said to him, "there must be a thousand students here."

"That's why we're here. We're going to have several assemblies. Then they're going to treat us to a real great lunch. A hot lunch. They want to show that they have great respect for us Marines."

Lieutenant Cooper put his arms up so that the voices would quiet down. He looked from side to side and waited as the simmering stopped. Now he had about 1,000 students ready to hear him.

"My name is Lieutenant Cooper. I'm with the Marine Corps. After I graduated from Annapolis Naval Academy, I could not have been more proud. We and our other armed forces keep this country safe from those who do not appreciate us. It's a big job. Our war ships are maneuvering oceans and seas. We are located at the embassies of many countries. We protect our ambassadors, along with our embassies. The responsibility is awesome. Our Marines were held hostage in Iran some more than twenty years ago. We are the few and the proud. Once a Marine, always a Marine.

"However, I'm not just here for the Corps. I'm also here for the Navy. The Navy teaches a lot of skills. You'll learn skills that you can take into civilian life. These are high paying skills. Pipe fitters that relate to sophisticated systems as a professional tradesman. Air Traffic Controllers, on our aircraft carriers, which is a high profile position. The job pays great when becoming a person with such a title. One thing many people never give any thought to is food management. As far as they're concerned they'll never starve." This brought on a great deal of laughter. "Hey, how about those restaurants people can't stay out of?" They were really into him with heavy listening. There were no signs of anyone being bored. He had them in the palm of his hand. "You also know you have an edge with the opposite sex. They love people in uniform. Why I've even had it pay off for me." There was a great amount of laughter, again.

"We need troops and we need them badly. How many of you have uncles and possibly aunts that served in our armed forces? Let me see your hands, please." A great many hands went up. "Well, well, well. Whether you realize it or not you come from very patriotic families. Your family members have helped keep this country free. You have no idea of how proud you should be of them. They served at the Battle of the Bulge, at Corregidor, Midway, Saipan, Italy, North Africa, at Bataan, and last but not least Iwo Jima. Then we had Vietnam.

"As I speak of these places in our military history, I get a big lump in my throat. We are a country of protectors. We are the guardians of the world. We lead the world in what we do. Now, I would like to get a good idea of how many of your graduating class or lower classman I can get to consider an enlistment with the Marine Corps or the Navy. For those graduating you can become officers. For lower classman you can become officers, as well. We have programs to make the best of enlisted men into officers. You can be extremely proud of yourself and what you are doing for your country. How many of you brilliant students are interested?" About 65% of them raised their hands.

"Oh my goodness. I can't believe it. I think this university is going to get mad at us if too many lower classmen enlist. There goes that great lunch we were going to get." The auditorium went into a rage at that one. Talk about success; they didn't come any more successful than Conrad. He was made to recruit.

CHAPTER
FIFTEEN

"Captain battalion calling. Yes, sir. Yesterday was the first day of the campaign and Lt. Cooper went to a university in upstate New York. I forget what the lieutenant said. They say he had them students under his thumb with a lot of humor. Well, if humor works, that's o.k. by me. I think it was wonderful that the commander kept up to date so quickly. I'm going to make it my business to meet her. Sir, I would appreciate it if you brought me along; if you should get that opportunity. He has what it takes for leadership. At this particular time he is being wasted as a lieutenant. How long has he been as a first? So far, he's been in the Corps two years."

"Major, he has done one great turnaround."

"How's that, Captain?"

"He got into quite a bit of trouble at Annapolis and he was determined to change the story. They didn't even let him graduate with his class. He got into a lot of trouble with two other middies. The commandant gave them new requirements to graduate. Out of the three, he was the only one that met those requirements."

So, the meeting between the New York City police and several other departments came about. Special agent Gus Malone, in charge of the regional office, chaired the meeting. Everyone was anxious looking at the conference table. Bruce sat next to Gus as Gus was looking at the chief.

"Chief Paterson, how much assistance did the NYPD give to the raid just above White Plains?"

"The location was in the city below White Plains. We were asked for several vehicles. The morgue assisted with taking three bodies in and assistance with some wounded lowlifes. Why didn't they notify us about the raid? We would have been better prepared for it."

"I'll second that,: said the police chief from Syracuse, New York.

"Well, Special Agent Prescott, why didn't you ask for their assistance?"

"For starters, sir, the locals don't really appreciate us because some of our agents have been less than polite with them. We have some bad apples that don't concern themselves about good liaison relations. But there is another point to be brought out here. It's called the bad cop theory, if I may, sir. We didn't want any leaks. They come about more often than can be appreciated."

"He makes a good point, Chief Paterson. That's the sad history with some in uniform in the city. There are always cops on the take. Your forces have over 30,000 uniforms and detectives. Of course, we're not excluded. We get bad agents, too. However, our screening process is more detailed. So, to a point I have to go along with Special Agent Forrest. I'm not looking to take sides; however, his points are well made. The same goes for Syracuse. Gentleman, I'll have to say this meeting is over. I apologize if there are any bad feelings."

CHAPTER

SIXTEEN

"So, Rachel, I hope you have had a better day today than I had. How did that first school go?" said Bruce

"Bruce, it went so well I have already notified the unit he's in. The news was too good to hang on to. And I must say, I made a great judgment call on that officer. My people have had a great time working with him. They had a nice warm lunch with the administration there and there were jokes about losing some of the student body. He had more than one assembly. The potential is for as much as one fifth of the graduating class to fill our ranks. They enlisted and some want commissions. So we have names and in a few months we'll be giving out those commissions. Isn't that great?"

Bruce looked dejected and tried to smile. He got up and walked over to the window, stared out and was troubled.

"Gus advised me not to let it happen again; but that I did a great job, otherwise."

"So, that should count for something. It's not that you're always on a raid."

"Rachel, what do you say to that engagement ring, now?" She had a big smile on her face. She looked down at her hands, and then looked up at the ceiling and then looked at him.

"I'd say that you're about to become an engaged man. My mother has asked about you. She wants to meet you. I told her not to push it. Mom said to me in a husky voice, 'I would like to have grandchildren, you know. Your brother is off in Europe going about business with his big band. He's too busy for getting serious with anyone. Rachel, you're it for us.' I told her thanks for the words. Is this an order or do I have any grace, here? So, with that said, it looks like we can go looking for that ring you want to so badly to buy to show that we're engaged to be married."

Bruce could hardly believe his ears. He went to her and put his arms around her and kissed her very slowly. He kissed her and kissed her. "Now, don't go telling me you can't breathe."

"Well, I'm just about out of breath. Sunday, we'll go to Mom and Dad and show her the ring. I want you to know you're not getting off too cheap. I hope you have a few grand available. I don't come cheap, considering that I'm thought of as a FOX," Rachel joked.

CHAPTER

SEVENTEEN

"How's my knee, Doc?"

The police surgeon was looking at his leg with a bullet wound. In running an errand to his bank a robbery was taking place. He declared that he was a police officer. Joseph Ferris was a traffic leader on the New York City Police Department. He supervised sergeants in traffic control, riots, parades and crowd control. He killed one person and wounded one as he exchanged gunfire, ending up being wounded in his knee and left forearm.

"Lieutenant, I'm going to have you on medical leave until I see some improvement. I'm going to give you an improved pain killer. You need to consider medical retirement."

Ferris became inflamed at the suggestion and demonstrated deep anger.

"Get away from me, Doc. In fact, stay away from me. You don't know what you're talking about. I've got 19 years on the force. A medical would give me a reduced pension and I don't want to retire, anyhow."

"Gee, Joe, I'm only doing my job. I don't have to take that abuse. I know you're hurting but it's my job to tell it to you the way it is. You need to also see the psychiatrist. I'm going to give notice to the chief that you should see the psych. Don't you ever explode like that on me again. I'll have you forced into your pension. Nobody treats me like that."

Joe Ferris and the Dr. stared at each other with flaming eyes. Neither one of them wanted to drop the stare. Joe finally broke it off and walked out of the office. He grumbled all the way out to his car. It was a beautiful day outside. But to Joe it was raining. He took no pleasure in the warmth of the sunshine. He held his wrist on the way to his car.

The campaign went to Harvard and then to Yale. His speeches were different in these schools. His audience was smaller and less of them.

He spoke to his recruiters in a low voice and said that his approach was changing. He looked at the audience. It was a coed audience.

"Hi people. I'm 1st Lieutenant Conrad Cooper. I hope you all enjoyed your lunch. The administration fed us troops and it was good." These lines always get the crowd relaxed and he is so good at it.

"I know that thinking of military service isn't the most popular subject going these days. With Iraq and Afghanistan at war, no one wants to hear about joining. Now, I have to bring about the facts of WWII. Churchill addressed Washington with helping the English out. That was what started the program called Lend Lease. My question to you is what do you think would have happened if Roosevelt had told Churchill that the war was not the problem of the United States? After all, our Navy wasn't in the best shape. We needed more ships and a better equipped army. Our army was still using WW1 equipment. Germany attacked Poland on September 1, 1939. Europe got shook up. You know what? Things would have been a lot different. We possibly may have lost the war and be taking orders from Hitler.

"Let me put this to you in a much more appealing way. This school is known for politics. How many of you would like to get into the United States House of Representatives; or how many of you would like to be in the rich man's club, the United States Senate? Military service is a big booster for gaining political office. It demonstrates sacrifice, selflessness and sincerity. I'd say that 90% of veterans do get to be politicians on the state and federal level." Attitudes were slightly different with that kind of thinking. He had struck a chord. Not as good as the patriotic speech but good enough. The bottom line was 10 students were giving it some thought.

CHAPTER
EIGHTEEN

Rachel's mother was watching her husband wearing a depressed mood. It was starting to feel a little heavy on her, as well.

"You have to pull out of that mood you're in. You're overdoing it."

"I am, am I. The doc is about to recommend retirement for me. A medical retirement. That would give us less money to live on. I'm going to the benevolent association and see if I can get them to look into it for me. Maybe they can get me on cold cases."

"Whatever. Just try to not think about it. As hard as it is on you, watch a ball game or something.

He gave that some thought and walked over to the television and put a game on and settled in.

Chapter
Nineteen

The restaurant was crowded as they made their way to their table. The waitress asked if they wanted a drink. They declined. "I've picked up a reputation as being disgruntled with the locals. The two law enforcement departments have never been the best of friends. The locals think very small of us. We're the glory grabbers after they have done all of the dirty work. It's pretty close to the truth."

"Bruce, lay low for a bit. I think you have been too active.

Why so many raids at one time? That strikes me as making room for inefficiency. I'm glad to say that we have had a good run for new troops. Connie is a natural for this type of work.

I'm surprised he hasn't hatched onto some foxy lady by now.

He is a handsome, strapping first lieutenant. He fortified my gut instinct. I'm so happy I gave him the opportunity.

"I'm bringing you to meet my parents on Sunday. You have no idea on how excited my mom is. She would like to know what you might favor as a meal. She is thinking of a roast. I really can't see anyone but a vegetarian not liking a roast."

"That's a no-brainer, Rachel. Does she ever make cherry pie for dessert?"

"Well, she's a cheesecake person."

"Say no more. I love cheesecake, as well." Bruce waved the waitress over. "We'd like to order now."

CHAPTER
TWENTY

The brass is always thinking about future events. As they see it Conrad Cooper is the highest caliber lieutenant there is. They do not want to waste his abilities. The meeting was between the battalion commander and the company commander. Regiment was on the phone. The ranks that were discussing him were as high as a full bird colonel. The lower two officers were on a conference call with the big boss.

"Gentleman," said the colonel, "this is really your ball game. If you think he has a decent amount of time in grade then go for it. If he has two years on silver go for it. I have more pressing work on my plate. This call is over for me."

"We thank you for your input, sir," the battalion commander said. There was a pause in their discussion.

"Captain, I'll give you a week to make a decision. How much time did you have in grade before you were promoted?"

"Four years, Major. He has half of my time. I'll think on it for the next couple of days and get back to you."

"I'd do it, Captain. We have a company commander leaving in about a month. He fulfilled his five year obligation."

CHAPTER

TWENTY-ONE

"Commander, how long will this campaign go on?"

"For as long as I can make it go on. I hate to say it but I believe I only have money for about a week left."

"That short, Commander?"

"Disappointing, isn't it?"

"How many campuses can we handle in that time frame, Commander?"

"We're going for five more. Logistics limit our options."

The battalion and company commanders meet again, but this time for a different purpose. "Captain, I don't like myself for what I'm going to do. The lieutenant is going to be promoted this afternoon. That's the part I take pleasure in. This is the part I now am going to take responsibility for that depresses me. I have a requisition for a battalion. This battalion, Captain, is ours. He takes command of Zebra company as of Monday. He is finishing up on this campaign just as we need him. Our battalion is on its way to Afghanistan. The Army and Marines, along with psychologists, psychiatrists and therapists, are being stationed all over that country. Needless to say, it is really a surprise to me. I wondered when we would see some of the war's unpleasant circumstances." The depression was quickly contagious as it showed on the captain's face, as well.

Chapter

Twenty-Two

Special Agent Bruce and the regional New York office Special Agent were on a conference call with Washington, D.C. Neither one of them was very happy. The director was chastising Special Agent Prescott. (*Washington now speaking*) "How long have you been with the FBI, Special Agent Prescott?"

"Nearly 21 years, sir."

"Nearly 21 years and you seem to not realize the politics of what you have done. When it gets to the director and he has so much on his plate, your issue is something no one appreciates. I'm putting you on notice. One more mishap on your part and we'll be asking for your resignation."

The director was very irritated with this. "It came through a congressman who is the chair of the committee that we fall under. It did not stop at the regional office. Your attitude, in this action, seems trivial to you. Not in Washington it doesn't. If I were you, I'd start thinking pension, now! You get my drift?"

"All too clear, sir, all too clear."

"Have a nice day, gentleman!"

"Well, I'm sorry this happened. I thought this was history, Prescott. You do know he is looking for you to call it quits now."

"Sir, would you be all right if I just hung on for another year?"

"Make it nine months and start breaking Mike in. He's got about 19 years, or perhaps I'll wait for about three months and discuss it with them. Just for the record, I feel they've gotten carried away. You have an excellent record, from where I sit. Let's feel our way through," said his boss.

Chapter

Twenty-Three

Bruce is at Rachel's headquarters chatting about the latest and both are in a sullen type of mood.

"I really never expected the campaign to have an ending quite like this. Cooper received orders that he is shipping out to Afghanistan upon his return to his unit. I was big time surprised. Tomorrow is his last stop in convincing students to sign up for the Navy or Marines. His unit goes to Kuwait and then ships to their new assignment. There is a whole new circumstance going into effect there," I told Bruce.

"Well," said Bruce, "today is a day of surprises. I'm on a banana peel with the FBI and soon no longer to be a special agent. Well, any wedding date to be set will have to be after I'm in a new position. Instead of waiting for the gauntlet to fall I'd better do some thinking."

"Would that mean that you possibly might relocate?"

"No, definitely not. I can't do that and marry you. What would you do if you were reassigned?"

"Well, I've got a good deal of time before anything of that nature happened for me. I just got here."

"What I need is a business I can move if you did move out. I could not stand not living with you. I may as well be in uniform, myself."

"Certainly, you can consider a security job. Possibly something of your own making. Bruce, you're not losing your job just yet. I know time flies, however, not that fast."

"At my age I would most definitely have to start my own business. I may consult with a planning agency so I don't waste time. I've got to put a handle on the circumstances." Rachel was very concerned for him. His situation caused him to look pale.

"I want to go to Mom's Sunday. Are you able to handle it. We originally planned to see her several weeks ago. Now, Dad is depressed with his wound and what the doctor stated. Between you, Lieutenant Cooper and Dad, Mom and I may have our work cut out for us."

Chapter

Twenty-Four

Mike came into my office and sat down. Mike doesn't need to be formal. We go back somewhere around 12 years.

"You caught flack from the raids and the locals, didn't you?" Bruce just nodded in acknowledgement.

"I'm due for retirement pretty soon. You have no idea how ticked off I am about the director. What I'm thinking is, if you have a mind to, we could get an agency going with both private citizens and the corporate world. Wake up, Bruce. We're both heavyweights. I'd just love to leave the Bureau."

"I'm looking into something just like you're talking about. And, of course, I'd love to have you aboard with me. I'm trying to get a handle on it now. Besides, I'd have to take you on as a vice president. Otherwise, I'd miss you too much."

"Besides Bruce, I have to keep hitting you over the head when you need it. So how is that gorgeous fiancée of yours? I'm tired of your talking about her; I want to meet her."

"When the opportunity presents itself."

Chapter
Twenty-Five

There they were, shaking hands vigorously, the law and order organization on the national level and the locals. Daddy and Bruce were smiling and happy to meet each other.

"I have to check you out, guy, you want to get serious with my kid."

"That'd a fine way to express it, Dad!" Rachel gave her father a slight dirty look as she placed her hands on her hips.

"I don't care how old you are, Rachel! You're still my kid. You're still my little girl. There was a time when you just ate that all up."

"Bruce, he's just impossible."

"He's being frisky. That's healthy."

"When do we get to meet your folks, Bruce?"

"You have to give it time. I just met you. I'd say about two months before anything serious happens. And that had better happen, if you get my gist."

"Oh, I know where you're coming from."

Mom comes around with her hands on her hips. She stares at the both of them. "Gee, Daddy. He's not going to run away from you. Not yet anyhow. Do you hear my stomach? It's telling me it's time to eat. Bruce, I made a very rare, succulent roast I know you're going to love. Two kinds of potatoes, sweet and scalloped. I hope you can appreciate some vegetables like spinach and corn. Daddy wipes them out real quick so don't waste too much time just staring at them." They strolled into the dining room and took their places at the end of the table.

The table being too long for only four persons, they just stayed at one end. Bruce was looking at the walls and the window dressings. He noticed a picture of Daddy with his uniform on when he graduated from the academy and another one with several other cops and one with his son that is in Europe with baseball gear for Little League. Then he looked at the table setting with one very wide grin.

"I'm in paradise, today. Mrs. Ferris, would you mind if I called you Mom?"

"Why I'd love that, Bruce, please do!"

"Mom, you've never met me until today. However, I could get used to coming here. This is a dinner for royalty. I for one am very grateful for it. It just looks so delicious."

"Why thank you, Bruce. Needless to say, you made my day. I could get used to compliments like that. Right, Daddy?"

"Yes, all compliments are deeply appreciated."

Bruce had the roast handed to him as he salivated and picked three nice slices. Then he started to eye the corn. "I just love corn and spinach. My goodness, Rachel, you must have advised your mother on everything I love to eat."

"Not really, Bruce. The Ferris family has always eaten like this. Daddy loves this type of food as much as you do."

Chapter

Twenty-Six

They were having coffee and a cigar in the living room. Then Bruce got an idea.

"Dad, can I call you Dad?"

"What's good for Mom is good for me. You go right ahead and call me Dad."

"I'm having an advisor check into things for me. He's looking at the security business. He's researching on how big the business is within a twenty mile radius, what the market looks like for residential as well as business. I believe there are a great deal of households that can support security for their property and might very well welcome it. I'm leaving the FBI shortly and I'm considering getting one established. If this should take place and I need to bring on personnel, do you think you might give some thought to joining my firm? If I'm not being too nosy, what kind of money are you making on the force?"

"Well, I'm on disability, just now; however, I was bringing in, as a lieutenant, $145,000 a year. Hey, I've got 19 years with the department."

"So, you're doing very well. I just thought I would ask. I'd only be able to bring you in at about $55,000 to start with, a far cry from your salary with the department. What are you going to continue to do if you go back to work?"

"Oh, I'm going back to work, all right, unless that doctor wants his head handed to him, I'm going back. I'll be working on cold cases. Most cops don't like working on cold cases. There's a great deal of work in it."

"Oh, well, it was just a thought."

"I greatly appreciate it, Bruce. It's an honor to be asked. Who knows what the future holds?"

Chapter

Twenty-Seven

Afghanistan, the country with their hands out--that's where Captain Cooper and his battalion landed. Why only a small group? It was a battalion with a specialty. It had linguist capabilities among other things. Something like a special forces unit. Several of the companies had such assignments for the mountain area. These troops were the extreme of deadly. They also were equipped with mine destroyers. Some of them were experts in disguise with capable accents for the different language groups. Their purpose was to become a member of the insurgents with their cunning abilities to be convincing. They went undercover as Afghans to be recruited by the Taliban or other. These troops are the pros that have had extensive schooling. The country made a very huge investment in their abilities. They were in the lower part of the country, closer to the war lords, away from Kabul. They had orders to be very friendly and slightly philanthropic. Excellent relations with the natives were paramount. They were equipped with several dozen MRAPS that were designed against being jumped. The roads were rutted and very crooked. They could mingle with these farmers because they were very poor.

A civilian organization was to follow to help the farmers with agriculture systems and convince the locals they should stop raising poppies and go into vegetables. For every poppy plant they could destroy on their farm they would plant two vegetable plants. They could possibly export the vegetable to the United States. Helping farmers to be happy with them was only half their goal. It was their hope to be recruited by the Taliban. Their disguises were too professional to penetrate. They had transmitters in their boots and belts to transmit positions. If they managed to get the unit attacked they would just have the opportunity to turn on the Taliban from within. Those that went undercover had many tanning sessions in a detachment prior to these orders.

Cooper's mission was plain commando tactics when receiving input to where the groups were hiding. It was realized that those making the penetration were at such high risk their lifespan with the insurgents might be only a half day. It all depended on their extensive skills of survival. They had to make sure they did not overact the part. To do their best, it was best to be silent and be without opinion among these suspicious people.

They called a conference for the company commanders on how their offenses would be. They had at least 12 exploders to clean the streets and save the men from losing life and limb. Between the carriers and exploders they were the safest of all troops. They were experts in tactics and Judo. In other words, they were deadly. They could be no less considering that the insurgents were extremely malicious. The fact was that they were not troops; they were murderers. They loved to behead their captives.

Chapter

Twenty-Eight

Bruce was looking into some of the established securities firms. He researched Wells Fargo and other well-known organizations. Instead of doing all FBI duties he was starting to use federal working time to his own benefit. He was thinking of sophistication in security products that would be installed with high price tag packages to more simple packages. He wasn't thinking singular. He was thinking of creating a franchise. He had saved a considerable amount of money and could also get a small business loan. He liked the idea of going big. He would set up contracts for those who joined his franchise to purchase all materials for companies he made contracts with. He would make the purchase of parts and systems and have a shipping department of one person to dispatch said goods and make a 40 percent profit on such shipments. The more franchises he was contracted for the wealthier he would be because he would contract with suppliers to lower the cost even more. The more he bought the cheaper the cost. He had to do his planning while being employed. He was getting just a little help from Mike. Mike was also thinking of his future without the bureau. He knew Bruce would do well with his salary. Hey, he was going to be the vice president of this company.

Chapter
Twenty-Nine

Rachel was pushing her recruiters hard. She was calling the high schools and asking for permission to send them in to speak with the senior classes. She was pushing the new G.I. Bill of Rights for Education. $3,000 bonuses were being offered for those enlisting. However, these men and women had to meet the qualifications of the Marine Corps Their standards were higher than those of the Army. They could be pickier due to the fact that they were a much smaller fighting force. What they had over the Army was prestige. That sharp-looking dress uniform did a lot of persuasion. Talk of famous battles such as Iwo Jima and the Battle of the Coral Sea got a lot of attention.

CHAPTER

THIRTY

Rachel decided to accompany her recruiters at these schools. Since she was considered a FOX she would attempt to put it to work. She advised her staff that she was going to make an extra effort. When she arrived several recruiters for both the Marines and the Navy saw why she decided to accompany them. They had the hardest time taking their eyes off of her. Her hair was down seductively, not her usual hair style. She gave more application, in a sexy way, to her makeup. She wore high heels rather than her usual uniform shoes. She also was slightly misbehaving. She could have gone on report. Her intentions were to be very persuasive with the male members of the graduating class. She made her way to the students and got real close to them. She also had a very light spray of perfume, for the male nostrils. She hated herself, in retrospect, but felt that it was for the betterment of her job. She was sorry, though, that she had not stayed professional for those under her command. She hoped she did not cause any damage in her leadership. She caused several of her staff to be desirous of her. They could have reported her to her boss. However, they also knew they would possibly be messing themselves up.

Rachel was ill at ease in her mind as well. *I'm a sinner just as much as the next guy. I feel like I'm selling myself. These young boys are drooling. I feel like a slut. They have 150 graduating males and I'll bet I can get at least 25 of them to sign up, or more.*

It turned out that she had 25 just for the Marine Corps They also recruited 35 more for the Navy, way beyond her expectations. Now, she had to get back to being the professional she was. She advised the few that were with her to be ready for supper at an Italian restaurant. She would meet them there at 8 o'clock. She wanted them in uniform because she wanted them to pass out cards as they left the restaurant. Of course, she was straitlaced at dinner and very Navy. She knew her staff was disappointed, now. They had enjoyed her wildness at the high school.

Chapter
Thirty-One

They were on their way to Mom's. She had confessed to Bruce on her misbehavior. He gave her a look but did not say anything. She advised that her being stupid actually paid off. She asked about how things were with his predicament. He advised as to what he was doing. She liked the idea.

"Wow, Bruce. That sounds exciting. But, it can take you away from me. What kind of marriage would we have?" said Rachel.

"I've thought of that, too. I would follow you unless you went where I couldn't go. I'd follow you and recruit more people into the franchise."

"That could work. I don't see myself going into any theater that you wouldn't be permitted in."

They were now at her parent's house. There appeared to be a rental car in front of the house. They pulled up behind it. "Maybe they're visiting a neighbor. I don't know the car.

But I wouldn't anyhow. I don't know what my mother's friends drive."

They got out of the car and went up the outside stairs. She rang the door bell and Dad answered and said there was a surprise for them. Rachel showed great surprise and walked in, with Bruce trailing.

"I don't believe it. It's my big brother Josh. Josh, is that really you?"

"Yes, I'm real. But look at you. You are so beautiful. And Mom told me about your career. I'm so proud of you."

He gave her a hug and squeezed her. "Let me look at you. Rachel, I wish I wasn't your brother."

Then Josh looked at Bruce. He shook hands with him and said, "You are one lucky son-of-a-gun. Do you realize how fortunate you are? I understand you two are engaged. Great! Rachel, Mom tells me you are a big shot. You have a very large staff of recruiters. You have had a very successful recruiting campaign. I have come home to wonderful news."

"And you, Josh--is there no one in your life? You're in your early fifties. What are you waiting for? You know, Mom's mad at the both of us. No grandchildren."

"I have met someone, Rachel. She's considering coming here. You'd make wonderful sisters. She is also a beauty."

"What are your intentions, Josh? Are you going to marry her?"
"I have to admit I probably will. I've had a few romances."

"Are you staying or returning to Europe?"
"I'm staying. I'm going to set up an orchestra, something like 15 musicians. That's what I've been doing all along.
Remember, I have a Master's degree in music.

Chapter
Thirty-Two

"I've made quite a lot of money traveling the countries. I have the best of musicians. Some of them may come here."

"You sound very promising," Bruce said.

"Dad advised me you are with the FBI. He also mentioned you may have a business concern coming up. I sure hope it's successful. I'll help in any way I can."

"Well, that's awfully nice of you. Gee, Josh, we're going to be brothers. I like that."

"I'll drink to that, Bruce."

"Hey you people, I've got a big spread on the table. Although with you guys, it won't be around very long."

"Josh, your mom is one of the best cooks in the world. She's cheating the world not having her own restaurant. Now, that would be a successful endeavor. My goodness, what a professional household this would be."

"Gee Mom," said Josh. "We could open a restaurant and have my orchestra as a house orchestra."

"You guys are dreaming. I'm too old to start anything like that."

Chapter
Thirty-Three

Explosions of IEDs on the roads is seen as a wonderful lifesaver of the troops. They are even hidden under human waste. Insurgents probably laugh themselves silly about the stench. That means no one will attempt to uncover the lethal device. However, in its explosion it does spread the stench extensively. Our troops get extremely angry when they have put on a fresh uniform. They send it to the laundry with a note; however, it doesn't really need a note. Some say why did the Lord have to make it stink so badly? The answer to that is that it is very toxic and needs to be gotten rid of. If it had a decent smell there would be no care about getting rid of it quick time.

The operator of this mobile device is happy with saving the lives of their fellow troops; however, they also become targets of the Taliban. The insurgents put a lot of time into trying to kill foreign troops.

THIRTY-FOUR

The compound for Captain Cooper's company is relatively quiet. He is in a waiting mode. One of his sergeants hands him a report and he starts to study it. The report is stating intelligence coming from a drone. They would be at a big disadvantage without the help of those units. They operate at 30,000 feet. The troops are guided by them for use in raids. A great many of the insurgents are killed and they recruit more Afghans by offering them a lot of money to join up with them. That's what happens when you have poverty-stricken farmers as far as the eye can see.

Speaking to his first sergeant Conrad says, "We have a raid coming up with Zebra Company. There's a group of 300 camped out at the south eastern border of Pakistan. What we have to do is get behind them, which means we go into Pakistan, on the lower ridge, and maneuver up behind the group of scum. Commando tactics are in order. We'll be using the neck-cutting wires. We've been training on the most precise way of handling the pressure. I want the wires nice and sharp. I want them to cut deep into the flesh of their necks to create as much pain as possible; but we don't want to get ourselves full of blood." The terrain was rockier than anywhere they had been. As they were cutting through what appeared to look like a short cut Cooper hears conversation. He manages a spot to spy on these killers. A group of hardened insurgents were laughing real loud. Coop motions to his men, getting in three positions and blast them away. When the time is ripe he yells, "Ya." They were shot down in two short minutes and never knew they were going to HELL in a matter of seconds. Coop looks at his men and says, "You guys are good. Now we'll get the others. This was just a warm-up."

Chapter
Thirty-Five

I need to see who is going to become a member of my new orchestra. I'll call Ziggy and Dutch, for sure. I think they'll join up with me. I'll say would you like to become a bandsman with the Josh Ferris Dance Orchestra. That sounds fancy. Somehow I think they're the only ones that will come. I've got to build this band with those that have jobs. They'll have to understand this band will not be a full time deal until we get established with recordings. Maybe I'll hold off on those calls. I'll just work with local people. Starting over is no piece of cake.

I'll place an ad in The New York Times and see what happens. Musicians that have an interest in being a member of a full orchestra of 15 people please call 212-338-2121. This orchestra will probably take on full time work within a year and a half.

I'm very fortunate to live at home, or should I say Mom's place.

CHAPTER

THIRTY-SIX

As Bruce and Rachel dine at the restaurant Rachel's most recent actions are about to come up.

"Bruce, I'm going to tell you something I'm not very proud of. But I have to tell you because it is heavy on my conscience." He stared at her and expressed wonder on his face. He saw her struggle with facial expressions, as well. She just kept on looking at the table and hesitated.

He speared a couple of pieces of lettuce, put them in his mouth and continued to stare at her. "Well, have you changed your mind about saying something or are you having a very difficult time beyond what you originally thought?"

"Several days ago I decided to join some of my staff and went to some of the high schools for possible seniors that might consider joining us."

"So, why is that such a terrible thing?" As she still shows a troubled pattern he says, "It goes deeper than that, eh."

"Yes, a little deeper than that. I decided to become unprofessional and put on a sexy front. You know, to get an interest in the mind of the guys. I wasn't military at all. I wore high heels and did not walk with a naval gait. I felt like a slut."

"Well, if you feel you sinned just ask for forgiveness. We both know you're a fine Christian woman. However, you did not look like one, right?"

"I almost got slightly flirty with them. I almost didn't check out the young ladies. The thing about it is that it paid off big time. I believe I got a lot of serious thinkers. Four guys signed up to enter the Navy upon graduation. And, to my surprise, a woman into the Marines, with the prospect of thirty-five guys and gals into the Navy and two guys into the Marines. The possible recruits feel safer in the Navy."

"Bruce, when am I going to meet your people?"

"You would have met them already if I didn't feel like such a prodigal son. I call a lot but I don't visit. My dad calls me the stranger. I've got two brothers and two sisters. Thank God they're not like me. I'm the oldest. They're all married. I've got ten nieces and nephew, a Christmas list that is awesome. I've attended three birthdays last year and my brothers got ticked because I didn't come around for the other birthdays. I did explain that it was because of my job. Maybe I'll call and we can see them over the weekend. You will have to prepare for a little sarcasm. You'll love Mom. She's like your mom. Dad wanted me to be a doctor. Two of my brothers made him happy. They're both G.P.s and my sisters teach at Princeton and Rutgers. One teaches Political Science and the other teaches theater. We will have a wall to wall sleepathon. It's hard to get that many siblings all together with a lot of rioting kids, especially the one called Bruce.

"I find myself short on good conversation. I have a hard time relating to their interests. Maybe it's because I don't have many interests of my own.

Chapter

Thirty-Seven

"What are you seeing foxy? Over."

"Bravery, I'm seeing vicious looking faces about a third of a mile from where I'm looking. They have all kinds of scars on their faces. I've been watching their guards. I'm going in closer to see if I can use my wire. I'm Mr. Silent. I've got the biceps to do it fast. Over."

"We seem to have a great spot. If we can do their Guards, which seem to be only two, we can catch them while they're eating and do them in. There are about 20 ugly members of the Taliban. They're going to have chow. Foxy and Bravery are moving in. Go for it now if it's good for you."

Sgt. Jones, also known as Gunny, who managed a transfer, feels his heart pounding in his chest. He moves up hiding and crawling. The guard is looking his way so he hides behind a tree. He also feels for his knife. He thinks back to training with the knife, spending at least two hours constantly throwing his knife at the targets that were set up. He was taught how to flip his wrist. During practice he flipped the knife continuously. He sees the guard partially looking in his direction. He runs out and the guard senses his run and smiles because he feels like he is going to pick a U.S. Marine off his feet. However, he can't outdo Jones. Bringing his weapon up to shoot, it seems he feels a sharp thud in his chest. He knows he's been hit and as he goes for the knife he gets hit with another in his throat. He became past tense. In Jones' excitement he smiles and feels proud because it went just the way he wanted it to go. He worked very hard on the targets to get a knife in the throat area.

Yes, silence is golden. He moved in and shot two as they ate. Firing was coming from everywhere. Oh, how wonderful the element of surprise is. Within 20 minutes they wiped out the group. These guys are what they're all about: Fast and furious.

CHAPTER

THIRTY-EIGHT

Battalion HQ is in a state of reverse orientation. The colonel is trying to put together all that has taken place up till the latest. The company commanders are enjoying coffee and whatever else.

"My, this coffee is great. How did it land up being here. Does the colonel have connections? Cookies and pastry, as well. Need you ask?"

"Don't let that get out, Captain." said the boss. "The men will not appreciate our pleasures. You have the goodies because of your responsibility in watching over all your men. Now, I would like a rundown of yesterday's actions. I understand one of your platoons had done some great work, yesterday. Please be as thorough as you can, Conrad."

"I emphasized some commando fighting, like using wires to silence the perimeter lookouts. I was orienting them to strangle fast and try to leave a nice cut for all to see. The Taliban are under the impression they are the big guys on the block. That strangling gets them shaken up. They love to behead and we demonstrate we love to strangle. I believe it gives us an edge in the psychology department. Two platoons went out with fever pitch. My troops are also using knives. Some of them are carrying two knives. Sgt. Jones took a picture in quick time with his unauthorized camera. I had to take it away from him. I told him you're not protecting yourself in the time it takes to do the shot. I have his photo here on his camera. He was doing a good job hiding it but I picked up on it. I'd like to circulate the photo of his work, if I may, sir?"

"Be my guest, Conrad." He took the camera up to his boss and as his boss looked at the photo he said "Gentleman, God bless Sgt. Jones. I have nothing but admiration for this Marine. Just look at that photo! This piece of garbage, lying on the ground, has a knife in the scum's throat and one in his chest. It's probably in his heart. Jones likes to make sure they're dead. At this time, Cooper, I want you to keep it to yourself, but this Marine is in line for a medal. He is getting one for gallantry. Gentleman, I love this photo. Anyway, I'm glad you took his camera away. It could have cost him his life. That's why we have the press here. Check to see how long he's been in grade. I'd love to have him pick up another stripe. I want him leaving here a five striper. Put another Marine in his spot for platoon sergeant. We're going to take the very best from each platoon that are handy with the blade and give that group special status. Let's have ten of them. Possibly two from each company. I love this idea. Have sergeant first class to be their platoon NCO."

"Colonel I'm hoping this is not going to go to his head."

"Nonsense, he's just a great fighter."

"Captain, I want a copy of that photo. You tell that Marine I want to see him."

"Yes, sir."

CHAPTER
THIRTY-NINE

Bruce was at a lawyer's office getting his business established. He took ownership of a franchise. He called it Prescott Security Services. He and Mike, his new minority partner, put together $40,000 of their own money and a credit line of 100,000 dollars. They set up an office with their products to be sold to franchisees. He had to have two convincing ads in The New York Times and U.S.A. Today. There would be a delay for the USA Today ad. He had to get his franchise established first. He advertised his services from his FBI background. This was to make it extremely appealing. How can anyone go wrong with being set up by these guys? Between the lawyer and some stock with two months' rent in advance they had burned through $8,000. Gee, Mike's investment was just about done. He was so happy that Mike decided to go in with him. These guys loved each other. They went back a long way and both had enough time with the Bureau to retire. They were proud of their little establishment. Now Bruce was also invited to Mike's home for dinner and Mike's opportunity to meet Rachel. Bruce already knew the family. They all prayed for him when he was on his assignments. Their office was not very far from Broadway. It had a good address with a decent rent. Bruce was getting to feel better considering how things went with the Bureau lately. He was looking for the exit sign. His career was now over because of a lack of contact with local law enforcement offices. His partner didn't think he did that well during his career either. He didn't do badly but not nearly as good as he wanted to do.

Chapter

Forty

Word had gotten back to Rachel about the happenings in Afghanistan. She had heard about Sergeant Jones. He was a star in the hat for Captain Conrad Cooper. Cooper's leadership was paying off. The newest commando group, now known as the "knives and wires" guys, had made a hit for their battalion. The colonel did not wait for the fight to come to them. His troops were swift and had very good intelligence working for them. You're only a success when you have the right tools.

She sent back word that she was so glad that she had the good judgment to have brought on Capt. Cooper, who was then a first louey, to work for her.

CHAPTER

FORTY-ONE

They got a call from Espirit Web Design. Seems they're busy designing internationally with more than one office. They have already had a leak in some of their data for special colors and diagrams. Their security people had egg on their face. They made arrangements to meet on Saturday 9 a.m. and look at their system. Bruce and Mike walked up to the front door and asked for Mr. Fisk. When the gentleman appeared it was uncanny. He had a slight resemblance to Bruce--same height and square jaw. Mr. Fisk looked at Bruce and decided a joke was called for. With a big smile on his face he asked Bruce why he ran away from home when he was ten years old. Bruce took up on it and said, "Mom always favored you."

Mike was hysterical, saying, "I don't believe it."

Bruce said, "Now you stay away from my women." The three of them were cackling.

Mr. Fisk shook hands with Bruce and Michael and said, "I'm very happy to meet you. I hope you can be of help."

Bruce said, "Well, the first thing we need to do is look at your present system. I assume you have tiny switches that are well hidden. Let's see how your trip switches are working."

"We have no trip switches. We have a guard that walks on a 24 hour basis. They check around the offices and the workshop."

"Mr. Fisk, I'm going to be blunt. You're operating in the first half of the 20th century. What does your agency charge you?"

"Four thousand a month."

"Well, we can help you with no trouble at all. However, it will cost you $20,000 for a system that will trip switches.

We operate with lasers that are undetectable. They work on the floor in an extremely thin layer to activate. They are on all your floors and are turned on for the night at 1/64 of an inch. These layers are very sensitive and will trip very easily. We have made arrangements with the local police to add your corporation to the burglary system. That will cost you $2,000 a month. We sign a contract with law enforcement to get 5% a month on that $2,000 dollars. Then we have cheaper systems, as well. It all depends on what you can afford. Whatever you would want we can set it up for you. When there have been kidnappings we advise these types of systems to the man of the house. This is my card. Give me a call when you have decided. We have a technician that will come out and set it up."

"I don't have to make up my mind. Bring your tech in as soon as possible. We're about to make an IPO on the stock market and we have to be in tip-top shape."

"Just as soon as we talk to our tech he'll contact you for installation." They shook hands and that was that.

CHAPTER

FORTY-TWO

As they walk out of the building they start to discuss the involvement of a technician. "I didn't know we had a technician," said Mike.

"We don't but it sounded good. The system I'm talking about is really simple. I read about it and looked into it. It gets put in tiny holes that are drilled right on top of the floor. It's a digital laser that splashes all over the floor when turned on. All the floors get them installed."

"So who's going to install it?"

"I'm going to check with Josh. That's Rachel's brother.

I'll make him a proposal. I've got the material and a video and ask him if he could make himself available for one to one and a half days. I'll pay him a thousand dollars to install it. I'll provide him with the tools and an ID Card. He'll have no sweat getting it done. I'll go as high as two thousand dollars. He can use the money big time. He's putting together a large group of musicians and I think he'll like the idea. He doesn't really need any special skills."

"How much is the material?"

"Two thousand, five hundred fifty dollars. We have possible eighteen thousand in profit that goes right back into the business."

"I like that, Bruce. That's good thinking."

"Yeah, I've been cheating the bureau out of some of its time. Since they have put me on notice of not being the kind of boss they want me to be, I have no qualms of making use of their time."

CHAPTER

FORTY-THREE

"Sgt. Jones reporting as ordered, sir."

"At ease Sergeant. Your C.O. Captain Cooper showed me the photograph. You do know I have promoted you?" said the colonel.

"Yes, sir. I thank you, sir."

"Captain Cooper made the photo available to me. I take it he returned your camera on orders not to use it again?"

"Yes, sir."

"Don't think taking a photo under such conditions is a bit like putting your life in danger; as though you don't have enough of that already?"

"Yes, sir."

"To me that photo represents commando skills that are badly needed. Have you received your orders from your commanding officer to recruit the men you want that have had the same training? This group reports directly to me for special missions. Between missions I want your men to practice, practice, practice. I want them to heavily develop the throwing of the knives at the heart and throat of the insurgents. You are now a five striper. I'm going to be dropping in on your training or should I say higher development as it goes by. I want to see the men in action. If there is anything you need don't hesitate to bring it to my attention. Your excellent leadership will be rewarded. I thank God that I have you among my troops. Now, this doesn't make you invincible, but it does make you great."

Chapter

Forty-Four

Josh is knee-deep in putting his fifteen band members together. He has met with five and was very pleased that they were very positive about being in his orchestra.

"Josh, you have a phone call from Bruce."

"Does he say what he wants?"

"Just get on the phone with him and find out." "Hi guy. This is a surprise call. What's up?"

"Have you ever worked with your hands in the manner of installing anything?"

"Why do you ask?"

"I want to make you wealthy."

"That's an excellent reason. You certainly have my curiosity."

"Do you think you or yourself and someone else can install a laser system that has an easy installation? It just looks a bit difficult."

"How about some particulars?"

"They are little laser units that are installed in tiny holes with the main unit going into a wireless box. It's activated from a security room. It throws waves onto the floor that get picked up by the police department. You need to go to the station and hand them a code and tell them the corporation it belongs to."

"As much as I would like to help you out, that's not me."

"How does $1,000 sound? It will take you two days or less."

"I still don't think I'm your man."

"I'll show you the package at my new store and raise you to $1,500. Is that a little more interesting? How about if I picked you up and brought you somewhere where we could have coffee and show you a schematic?"

"You have to do better monetarily."

"Seventeen fifty sound better?"

"Two thousand sounds a lot better and maybe not then."

"I have to admit I'm surprised."

"I did work with my dad on installing a couple of items, but not of this nature."

"It's not a difficult operation or I would not have called you. You're good, Josh. My hat's off to you. I thought you could use the money for your band overhead."

"I'll look at the schematic. I had blueprinting in high school. If I do this for you, it's going to cost a minimum of two grand and possibly two and a half grand. Nothing is as simple as people say. I'm not out to give you difficulty. To take me away from what I'm doing in getting organized, that's the kind of money I'll want. I'll bet a tech would charge you no less than $3,000 or more. Why don't you install the system?"

"Because I wanted to give the impression I had a staff. If you feel you would not be efficient enough for the job I'll have to do it myself."

"Let's see the sketch of the job and I'll tell you. I also don't want to waste your time, Bruce."

"Are you available tonight? I can pick you up at 7:30?"

"Works for me."

"Great, until then," said Josh.

"Bye."

Chapter

Forty-Five

"I spoke to Josh and showed him the schematic. He is doing the job. Mike, he really surprised me. He is great at bargaining. He dropped the profit by a thousand or more. I'll have one sharp brother-in-law. It runs in the family. Rachel took right after her father and brother. That's why she is where she is. I'll have to advise her on how Josh broke my horns. He's is going to make that music group profitable. He told me he picked up a Master's degree in Italy."

"Master's in what?" "Business and Music."

"Mike, I have to sit with the boss for a few minutes. I think it's about Washington's scorn."

CHAPTER

FORTY-SIX

"I've got a bad feeling," said Captain Cooper. "Real bad. Let's look over that ridge." His platoon is signaled to scatter. As they approach they don't like what they see. There are fifty Taliban guerillas. They returned to Cooper and advised him.

"There's about fifty of them, Captain."

"Well, that's a lot but we outnumber them," said Cooper.

"Plus we have the element of surprise. Gunny, take ten men and try to flank, if possible, in a very quiet on your toes manner.

Corporal Redding."

"Yes Sir. Make another flank, if possible, to their right. We'll take out the ones closes to us. Be prepared to use your wires and knives. Hey, if they're dead before we walk in on them, the safer we'll be. We might be able to reduce the numbers by killing quietly. Every one we kill quietly is one we don't have to fight. Lt. Blake, take your platoon to the farthest flank, quiet and steady. I have got to have the sharpest knife in this outfit. I'm in a dagger throwing mood!" said the commander.

Gunny moved in like a snake. He went in quite a ways and saw his first victim. He was taking in the sky and the stars. He placed his right hand, as he held his weapon with his left arm and massaged his neck. Little did he know what was going to happen to his neck. At this time, it was prime real estate. The Gunny pulled on his wire and started to laugh under his breath as he was crawling up on Mr. Taliban. His wire had been sharpened so that he could gut the neck. The next tough guy would get the double daggers. The execution needs to be at the speed of lightning. He slithered and stood and wrapped his weapon around the hombre's neck with a lightning pull. Shock took the hombre and as hard as he tried he could not get his fingers under the wire as one of them was cut to the bone as blood was coming out. The Gunny gave the wire a loosed jerk for as much pain as he could deliver. His prey was falling to the ground. *That went better than I could have imagined it.* The guard didn't even have a chance to gurgle. His Marines were moving out from all positions. They took out ten scarf heads without creating a ruckus and he started shouting under his breath and communicating with his platoon leaders. They hit the jackpot. They cut thirteen throats and took 23 prisoners with them. They marched them with their weapons very close to their heads. They brought them to intelligence where an area was created and had their local prison camp. One Marine lost his cool and strangled a prisoner. Cooper went to the Marine and whispered in his ear, "I should court martial you. You know that."

"Yes, sir." said the Marine.

"However, I really enjoyed your beating on him."

Chapter

Forty-Seven

Bruce and Mike were checking the inventory in their new store to be right on top of it all. This is what they called running an efficient operation. The phone rang and Bruce advanced to it.

"Prescott Securities Services, can I help you?"

"Bruce, it's Josh Ferris. The brother of your heart's desire."

"Well, that's one way to put it, I guess. Did you finish the job or do you have a problem?"

"The job is done. I had several problems but nothing I couldn't handle."

"How long were you at it?"

"I would say 11 hours. I gave the clientele brochures and a rundown. I might say he was very impressed with me. Now, you are indebted to me to the tune of $3,350. I thought I'd give you a break. I could have charged you a full $3,500, considering a possibility of our becoming related to each other. When can I expect the check?"

"I will send it out tonight. I'd appreciate it if you would call them in say, about 2 days and see if they are having any problems. If they are I'll go in and fix whatever needs fixing. I appreciate your taking on the job. You probably saved me about $1,500. Every little bit helps right now. Thanks, big time."

"You're welcome, Bruce. Take care."

"I wonder if he would do it again, considering he did a good job. He could make money and we could save money."

The phone rang again and Bruce again picked it up.

"Prescott Security Services. Can I help you?"

The voice on the phone stated that he would like to speak about securing his estate. The estate is three acres and needs a couple of monitors and lasers for trip signals.

"Where are you located?"

"On Mt. Carmel Avenue in Little Italy. It's a dead end and I'm on the end. My name is Jimmy De Chaimo. I have a very large restaurant that does catering, as well. I live 200 feet perpendicular to the restaurant."

"Would 7 o'clock be all right with you?"

"Yea, that's good."

"See you then."

Chapter

Forty-Eight

They're at a new restaurant with tinge of high class. They're taking in the surroundings with quite an interest. Rachel is pointing out a couple of architectural structural combinations. "I wonder what their security system is all about."

"Speaking of security systems, I had a business deal with your brother." The waitress asked if they're ready to order. Checking the menu he says. "I'll have the Delmonico Steak," and Rachel orders the leg of lamb. The waitress goes to place the yummies. "Your family certainly has its share of smart genes."

"Well, all families would like to think that, wouldn't you say?"

"Josh installed a security system for me the other day. I was already to offer him $2,500 as a maximum. Well, he gave me a great demonstration of how he does business without the music. I thought to engage him at twenty-five hundred and he had a heftier bill of three thousand three hundred fifty dollars. He took into account any and all problems; of course the hours, which went into overtime, between two days, amounting to something over ten hours." The waitress returns with their order and Bruce eyes that steak and salivates.

"Why did you bring Josh into something of this nature? He doesn't lend to it."

"Because I figured he could use the money, considering the project at hand with his music organization. He could certainly use an infusion of money. I still saved some overhead, just not as much as I thought I would." He takes a slice and his eyes go up partly up. "Oh, what a delicious steak."

"I hope you have no ill feelings about it."

"Not at all. He's just a good businessman. I take it that orchestra he is putting together is going to be a successful endeavor. Rachel, let's go see my parents on Sunday. I'll call and advise that we're coming over. I certainly hope I don't give my dad a stroke. Be ready for busting from my kid brothers. I feel also a successful business coming up with Prescott Securities Services. Would you marry me nine months hence?" He gives her an intense look. She says nothing and looks at him.

"Well, would you?"

"Yes, I'll marry you, now that I know who you really are. I do love you very much. Now that you brought that tremendous subject up, we're going to be two very busy people on top of your being busy with your new business. Of course, there is lots you are not involved in. You certainly have gotten off into an excellent start.

"Mom will be so elated. She won't know how to contain her excitement. She'll be verbalizing nonstop at the church. We'll be married at the Church of the Redeemer in Astoria. My brother had better give us a break on his newly minted orchestra; or I'll lay one on him. I'm hoping, perhaps, he'll accept about fifteen hundred."

"I'm certainly happy I have a new credit line. I'm going to start advertising for franchises, even though I'm just starting myself. They're going to have to buy my products and I'll do all the advertising. I believe two months from now I may possibly make the FBI happy and retire. I know they're waiting on me for the news. All of this for not advising the locals on our raids. Pity, pity and more pity. For shame. For shame. Bye-bye and good riddance. And Mike feels the same way."

CHAPTER
FORTY-NINE

"I got a call from the regiment yesterday. I filled the colonel in on what has taken place since we have arrived. I advised him about the new squad working with wires and knives. Well, I got a pat on the back for that. That very seldom happens. I told him we have been very constructive in getting rid of these guys."

Meanwhile the wire and knives specialists were going at the scarves with a vengeance. They got addicted to the sound of their knives cutting flesh. The harder they threw the knives the better the sound. The first target was the throat and they never seemed to miss. Therefore, the second knife wasn't necessary but it felt good to throw it. They did in two squads of the scarf heads. They also fell upon a cache of weapons. There were about 100 AK47s, 200 grenades and six thousand rounds of ammunition.

As the colonel spoke his sergeant major asked for a word with the colonel. They quietly spoke to each other. The sergeant major then left the tent.

"I just love these guys. Two of them got minor wounds. I want each company commander to send a squad down to the border. They found a cache of weapons and ammo. We need to get that under cover of darkness if they don't get it first. Once we get it it can't be used against us. I have intelligence that just inside the Pakistan border they are running businesses and using that profit for their purchases. None of the locals know who they are. They keep a very low profile not to give themselves away. I would like a platoon to be air dropped over there. It will have to be a night drop. Infiltrate the area and keep their ears and eyes open. I'm going to suggest a group of Army Rangers too, from their 82nd or 101st division drop down there. These troops need to look like Pushtans. What we also need are Marines and the Army to learn the language. We badly need that for infiltration. This should have been thought of a long time ago. Captain Cooper, what's your take on what I'm saying?"

"The trouble is, Colonel, I'm wondering if it's too late. If it isn't I'm gung-ho for it."

"You see, Cooper stills knows how to do some browning." That broke up all in the tent. That was considered a lighter moment.

CHAPTER
FIFTY

The shrubs were as tall as forty feet with a very fancy swirling of architecture. The garden was quite considerable with white, black and red roses. It also had gardenias, orchids and lilies. There was a tennis court and a brook running from the side to the middle and back to the side again several tiny bridges on the landscape. It had a four car garage, with a stone driveway in a horseshoe shape. There again were flowers alongside the garages. Rachel was in awe. She could not believe what she was looking at. She felt like her jaw had dropped. She looked at Bruce, as he had a very serious look on his face. He knew what she was thinking. *He comes from wealth without him acting like a wealthy person.*

"Tell me this is not your dad's house."

"O.K. it's not my dad's house. Remember I told you my brothers are surgeons and my sisters are professionals. Dad put five children through college. Yet, my grandparents were not rich people. Dad did this all by himself with some help from Mom. Mom is a judge. They're very loving parents. Don't concern yourself with the wealthy environment. My parents are down to earth people. They just don't believe I cannot get away as often as they would like me to. They're all married and that makes me feel out of place lots of times. I never hear the end of what's keeping me from getting married. They say you're tall and handsome and well educated. You're just chicken, puck, puck."

"Are they all here today? I can't wait to meet them. Really."

"Mother there is a strange car in our drive way. I take it that's Bruce. Mother, it's no mirage, it is Bruce. He's opening the door for his lady in waiting. Mother, she is gorgeous. A man can take all the time he wants when he brings home a gorgeous creature like this lady. What beautiful grandchildren we have coming up."

"Daddy, she is beautiful. I'm as excited as I can be. This house is going to be filled with beautiful women. I can't wait; I'm going out to meet them."

"Wait for me, Mother."

Bruce is looking around catching up environmentally. The garage door went up and there stood the surgeon and the judge, his parents. His mother went to him and Rachel.

"I'm Bruce's mother and you're Rachel, I gather."

"You gather right, Mrs. Prescott."

"Well, you guys are engaged so you can call me Mom."

"Thank you so much for that, MOM."

"Bruce, she is darling. What a gorgeous woman you have brought home. Daddy is drooling." His father comes right after his mother.

"Hi Dad, how are you?"

"How can I be when you bring home such a beautiful woman? Rachel, I am delighted to meet you. So you're doing Bruce a favor and marrying him? Huh."

"I'll say one thing to you, right now. I'm am so happy to meet you. I cannot believe how charming Bruce's parents are."

"So, Bruce when is the big day going to be?"

"Dad, if all should go well you can figure on a year. Hopefully."

"Come on in the house. Your brothers are here. When we came out they were sitting in the family room having some wine."

Bruce could see them out of the corner of his eye. They were waving and signaling all to come into the house.

FIFTY-ONE

One brother says, "We're Bruce's older brothers." Then Rachel had a puzzled look on her face.

Then Bruce said. "See, what did I tell you? They're two busters. They're my kid brothers and they act like a couple of kids. They have no sophistication. And yet they're in the medical field."

The other brother says, "Mom, you do realize we have a cop in the house?"

Mom says, "Goodness, that's right. We have an FBI Special Agent in our midst."

"Mom, then you wonder why I don't visit as often as you would like me to. I have two stand up comics for brothers and I'm a cop when I come here."

"Well, to make you feel better I have steak, roast leg of lamb, sausages, Caesar salad, vegetable and spinach soup, with a desert of cherry pie, pumpkin pie and strawberry cheesecake.

We also have wine, beer and liquor and coffee and demitasse.

"I'm full already, Mom."

The sisters-in-law came in from the garden and quickly introduced themselves.

Rachel was so busy talking to the women she would come to know as her sisters-in-law. She was having a wonderful time.

"My fox, I'm thoroughly exhausted. Right now, I could get arrested for driving under the influence. Well, just as long as I drive without wavering I'm all right."

"Your family made me feel very important today. They showed me so much love; I was overwhelmed."

"Yeah, my mother said it was worth the wait. The family is crazy about you. But not as crazy as I am. You know that big house is very much needed when all the grandchildren are there. I would say there will probably be around a dozen of them."

"Bruce, I don't really want a large family. I'm just not the type."

"You won't get an argument out of me. One or two kids, at the most."

"I'm glad you feel the same as I do. After I said it, I wondered what your reaction was going to be."

"Rachel, you're in safe waters."

CHAPTER
FIFTY-TWO

"Mike, read my copy for the ad I'm placing for franchises."

"This is good. I think you've been wasting your time with the Bureau."

DREAMS CAN COME TRUE WITH "PRESCOTT SECURITIES SYSTEMS". ATTEND ONE CLASS FOR AN ORIENTATION AND YOU'RE ON YOUR WAY. I WILL SUPPLY WITH ALL SECURITY PARTS AND WILL DO THE ADVERTISING. YOU WILL BE FOLLOWING IN THE STEPS OF A SPECIAL AGENT OF THE BUREAU-- THE BUREAU THAT KEEPS YOU SAFE.

"We're going to be running a full page ad for two weekends. It's going to cost $1,500 that was saved having Josh do the installation job for us. Mike, we have to work tomorrow night and Thursday night, and Saturday. We have two customers for Saturday. We've been at it for three weeks. I'm hiring a part-time installer. He'll work two hours an evening and Saturday. If he gets bogged down we'll get another part-time installer. We'll pay $20 an hour with the possibility of coming aboard with us. I took the privilege of running an ad already. I can cancel it if you're not comfortable about it."

"Bruce, I'm beginning to feel like I'm not pulling any weight. You have this whole thing moving right out. I'm beginning to think I'm a silent partner."

"Perish the thought. I'm the one on the threshold of being pushed out. I'm resigning in another month. The boss upstairs got some heat from Washington last week. He asked me if I've looked into anything as of yet. He felt very bad. He told me they want me out. I'm not politically correct. So I'm going as fast as I can, which makes me look like I'm doing all the work. You'll be doing a good share when you're ready to split. "$6,000 a month is pretty good when you are working. When we're doing a full week and we're both at it I think we'll be pulling in about $60,000. It's not great but it's not bad. When we're somewhat mature in the business, it will be somewhere at $120,000. That should take something like two years. There seems to be something about me that makes people say 'YES'."

Chapter
Fifty-Three

The colonel decides to write a letter to the joint chiefs of staff. He is asking the general to consider, if he would, SPECIAL FORCES to drop into Swetta, with support personnel, with disguises of the Taliban with knowledge of the Pushtan language. There is a concentration of business groups that are making money in the marketplace, which is very large, and using those profits to fight the war. To dry up that area of Taliban business, they must keep a very low profile, so that they are not realized to be other than Pakistanis. The Pakistanis must not know about these troops because it might be leaked to the press. If this strategy could be brought into force if may save many lives, including in other parts of the world. To overlook such an action may be perilous for our troops in Afghanistan. Perhaps the secretary may find this to be constructive.

Thank you,

Colonel Josiah James
U.S.M.C.

CHAPTER
FIFTY-FOUR

Rachel is on her way to one of her recruiting stations at Times Square when she sees a woman that resembles a former classmate in high school. She is window shopping with a boyfriend or husband, possibly a fiancé. She has to say hello or it will drive her nuts for a day. She slowly approaches the couple and makes a loud call with the woman's name. "Janice Alexander." The woman turns around and looks at Rachel with a stumped look on her face, saying to herself that she doesn't know anyone in the Navy. Rachel says, "It's Rachel Ferris, Janice. We went to high school together." Both Janice and the gentleman look at Rachel. Then Janice says, "Why Rachel, how are you? I had no idea you were in the Navy. You look wonderful. It agrees with you. How long have you been in the Navy?"

"I have thirteen years of service. I hold the rank of Lt. Commander. I told you gals I was going to Annapolis when we were in our senior year. I'm not surprised you don't remember; so much was going on with so many of us talking about where we were going to go to college. How are you doing? Aren't you going to introduce your friend to me?"

"Rachel, excuse my bad manners. You have taken me by surprise and have just about left me speechless. This is my husband, Ronald MacKenzie, Ron Mac, for short."

"I'm very pleased to meet you, Ron."

"As I am pleased to meet you. What do you do in the Navy?"

"You see that recruiting station there?"

"I'd better be able to see it or I have a major problem."

"I'm their boss. I'm the commander of all the Navy and Marine Corps stations in the greater metropolitan area. Yep, they all have a female boss."

"My hat is off to you, Rachel. I see you are engaged. It's a beautiful ring."

Rachel lifts up her hand to show it to them. "Thank you, thank you very much."

"When's the big day?"

"We haven't set a date, but it will be about a year from now. Janice!"

"Yes."

"I just got a crazy idea."

"What might that be?"

"Would you consider being a bridesmaid for me? It would be like old times. Give it some thought, would you?" Rachel has an imploring face and slightly bends down to implore her.

"Please think about it. That's all I can ask. I'd be so grateful to you."

"Janice, give that some thought," said her husband.

"Here, take my phone number. Two phone numbers. My office and my mother's. If you could make it, I'd love to have you both over for dinner. Then you could meet my future husband Bruce Prescott."

"My Rachel, that's a fancy surname you're picking up. Prescott. It's classy."

"Why thank you. I'll be sure to mention that to Bruce. Please call me."

"I make sure she does, Rachel. I'd like to see her in you bridal party. And I look forward to meeting Bruce. Here, this is our telephone number. I think it's a great idea."

"Well, it looks like my husband has made my mind up for me. Isn't he great?"

Chapter
Fifty-Five

"I suggest you take 10 days' vacation and 15 days' pay in lieu to add to your first year of pension, which would give you about $60,000. I want you to know I would have voted for you to stay right where you are. You're really too good a special agent to lose. They're living in a different world. They have made hay out of nothing. Those locals would be very disappointed if they knew it cost you your job. I've got 25 years of service and I'm extremely disappointed in them. I have been offered spots on board of directors for Fortune 500 companies. At least three of them have asked me to join them."

"Are you seriously thinking of joining them?"

"Just between the two of us, yes, I am. I could be in your shoes some time myself."

"You know something, if you should go forward with what you're telling me, would you possibly help me out?"

"I'd help you out in any way I could!"

"I'm in a new business part-time. I'm running a franchise for securities. I'm advertising as we speak. I have been working evenings taking orders and I'm bringing on help for installation.

I'm doing much better than I anticipated. Perhaps if you would make a recommendation for my services with any company that you might deem needs to improve the security system..."

"Bruce you can consider that done. I'm going to sorely miss you. Why don't we keep in touch? I'd like to give you a call on how things are going for you. If I should get onto several boards, I'll do the same thing on all of them. Now, that wouldn't mean that anything would come from it; it just means that I will make it an issue. That's the best I can do."

"Well, boss. I couldn't ask for more than that."

"Hey, how's Rachel doing?"

"You do know we're getting married?"

"No, your engagement I knew about. When are you getting married?"

"In the space of a year."

"Don't forget to invite me. You would probably have had me there if you were still with us, you know."

"I do want you to be there. Very much so. She's going to have her old boss from the academy there. He's why she is where she is. O.K. then, put in the necessary papers and we'll get the show on the road. I'm going to miss you like she misses her old boss. She always considered her Navy father. But I will not get gooey with you. Besides, I'm too old for that, anyhow."

CHAPTER
FIFTY-SIX

"Sir, I received a request from the colonel of that Marine battalion that would need the earth to stand still. He doesn't seem to realize what he is requesting."

"And what would that be, General? That you order the Army to place commando troops to fall into Stretta because Taliban business units are keeping a very low profile and aiding in the cost of the war? He's talking about commandos and support units."

"It seems to me he has Afghan fever. You tell him request denied. It wouldn't be a bad idea if he called one of those shrinks in. I may just relieve him of his command. I don't believe I want him there anymore. General, send in a new commander to replace him. He has too much imagination. I can't afford to have him there. Contact him and advise him he is being relieved of his command. Get one of your best to replace him. Give the new commander an immediate order to ship out. Then I want you to send someone to see his wife. This is going to be a blow to the both of them. The woman will need comfort. I want you to keep in touch with her. Offer her things to lighten life for her, things to make life easier for her. If necessary, have meals catered to her for several months. We owe it to him. See if you can fly a family member to be with her. These families have made a tremendous sacrifice. We're Marines. We take care of our own."

"Right away, sir," said his aide.

CHAPTER
FIFTY-SEVEN

She put a roast in the oven and started chopping up lettuce, carrots and broccoli and placed them in a bowl. She'll place some oil and bread chips on the side and they'll have a great salad. She threw some regular and sweet potatoes in the oven with the roast. Everyone would be here for a 7 o'clock supper.

There was a knock at the door sometime later and it was her former high school girlfriend turning bridesmaid.

"Hey you guys, thanks for coming. Dinner will be ready in about twenty minutes. Would either of you like a glass of wine? It's nothing much, I very seldom drink."

"Hey, I'll have a glass," said her guy.

"It's burgundy," said Rachel

She brought out two glasses of burgundy and they were delighted. "Bruce should be here any minute now. Just make yourself at home and relax."

The knock was at the door for the failing FBI agent. She excitedly goes to the door and opens it, saying, "Bruce, they're here for dinner and we're going to have a grand time."

Before she even goes to introduce him he goes to them and shakes their hands. "I'm so happy to meet you. I'm Bruce."

"Ron Alexander, and very pleased to meet you as well."

"And, you're Janice. How are you?"

"Why, I'm very well, Bruce. Rachel, he's a handsome guy."

"Did you hear that, Rachel? She says I'm handsome. Well, for a handsome guy she sure gave me a hard time."

"Let's not go into that, Bruce. Time to sit at the table. I'm bringing in some shrimp for an appetizer."

"Shrimp," said Ron. "I'm going to have a delightful time here tonight."

"Well, that's why we are getting together to have a good time and talk about the wedding."

"Rachel, this shrimp is so big, love," said Bruce.

"Nothing but the best. I have such a delicious roast I'm about to cut up, with a delicious salad."

"Do you feed like this all the time, Rachel?" said Ron.

"With my job I really don't have time to cook. My love here takes me out a lot. But, we have to reduce the eating out somewhat to save money. Excuse me while I go get the roast.

I'm starting to drool."

"Having a roast, we're all drooling," said Beatrice.

As the evening went on they were in a joyous mood. They all loved each other. They decided to get at least one more bridesmaid, if at all possible. Beatrice advised that one of the other girls lives around the neighborhood, somewhere. The problem is she probably is married and has a new surname.

Chapter

Fifty-Eight

A helicopter is flying overhead as the colonel looks up. He's puzzled. He is not expecting anyone. It sends some items on the ground flying around as it touches down.

The door flies open and a colonel comes out and gets the surprise of his life. His replacement alights from the jeep and says hello to the colonel and hands him a paper. The colonel looks at the envelope and opens it up. He starts to read it and starts to have a fit.

"What's the meaning of this, Colonel?"

"It is self explanatory, Colonel. There's no need for me to explain. I was sent here to take over your command.

You're to be out of here at first light is what the commandant explained. Whatever your problem is, you're to take it up with the commanding general of the Corps. I've have been given such a short notice of this assignment. Do I look happy to be here? This has caused me a great deal of discomfort which is something I'm not free to get into. I believe it would be best to call battalion personnel into a meeting and advise that you're being relieved of your command."

The colonel is standing in shock and feels great humiliation.

"I cannot for the life of me understand what's going on. I have to report to the corps commandant. Why do I get the feeling my career is not going to get anywhere?"

CHAPTER

FIFTY-NINE

The colonel has returned to the states. The new colonel strikes all as being sad. *Martha, my love, you don't deserve this. I'm beginning to think about leaving the Corps. It's too much of a hardship on you. You don't deserve this. I've got 23 years of service and I'm leaving. I'm going to retire. It isn't worth it just to make brigadier. My concern is your well being. When I return I'm putting in for my pension. Then we'll do some traveling. Just the two of us.*

As the colonel's wife reads the letter she is crying. *Colonel, you have no idea how wonderful that sounds. Of course, I too was hoping you would leave as a brigadier. That certainly was your dream. It will be delightful to travel. Just the two of us. Your letter has me fortified. Gerald is coming home from Cornel to stay with me until you come home. I tried to talk him out of it but he would not hear of it. Well, he's only got one year left, anyhow. Rest easy Joseph. Things will be all right here.*

Captain Cooper gets a phone call. The first sergeant advises him that Colonel Joseph Spears is on the phone.

"Yes Colonel."

"Captain, why is there a detachment to this battalion?"

"Our former commander took ten Marines and made a special unit out of them. They reported straight to him. They're commando specialists. They specialize in knives and choking wires."

"I would like you to come to headquarters. Let's talk about these killers of yours. I'll see you at 2 hundred hours."

"May I ask the colonel what's up?"

"You'll find out."

"The new guy wants to talk to me. Who knows, maybe he'll make me a major," Cooper states in humor.

CHAPTER

SIXTY

Cooper took the helicopter over to his new boss. He looked around the compound for any changes that came about. The guard came to attention and presented arms and Cooper returned the salute. There he was, his new boss, smoking a pipe and looking out the window.

"Captain Cooper reporting as ordered, sir."

"At ease, Captain. I'm trying to get the lay of the land and troops. These ten Marines that are extremely deadly--what brought the special group about being led by a gunny sergeant?"

FROM THIS POINT ON IT GETS MORE DEADLY THAN IT EVER WAS BEFORE

The gunnery sergeant moved around like a snake. He spotted a sentry guarding the group. He had to decide whether to use a wire on him, which would cut into his neck, or take him down with knives. He did a remarkable job. As he snuck up the guard happened to turn his way. Too late for the choking wire. He sent a blade into the insurgent's chest and very quickly followed up with another blade into his neck. Mr. Taliban came down pretty quickly, without making noise. This was repeated several times by other Marines in this attack. We had fifteen prisoners.

At the colonel's office it's a different story. "What I want is all the companies under my command to be deadly. If it's possible, let's have a night invasion with a lot of sneaking up.

"I really love the knife in the throat. Let's do the knife in the throat with day attacks and the wires at night. I'd also like, if possible, the arm pulling back the neck and a blade shoved into their backs. And with that a little twist of the blade. I want these pieces of garbage to really feel a great deal of pain on their way to Hell. We need to be proactive with excellent intelligence reports."

"Who does intelligence work?" asked the boss.

"I'd have to look into that, sir. To be quite honest, I really don't know."

Then the assistant commander advised, "Three men in Captain Rogers' platoon. He commands Able Company. However, sir, we could use newer equipment to work with. Presently we're not that good with intelligence."

"I'm sorry to hear that," said the boss. "Intelligence is very vital to operations. Contact Washington and see what you can come up with," said the boss.

"I'll be on it the first thing in the morning, sir." The major nodded his head.

"We don't wait for them; we go after them. Since they are always threatening the Afghans with having their heads cut off, I'd like to leave them with a lot of knife wounds. Deadly knife wounds. This way we can proactive without shooting as much and having our guys get wounded or killed. Let's be night stalkers. No. Let's be deadly night stalkers. I think it's one way to hold our casualties down. I'd love to throw the fear of God into them. I want them to be afraid of us. Really afraid of us. Your men should be back to your unit no later than tomorrow morning. That's all, Captain."

Chapter

Sixty-One

"So now you're leaving the feds, eh," said Ron

"Yes, I'm turning businessman in the security world. I'm starting franchises. I'm already advertising for them. I will shortly be out of the Bureau as a retiree. My Bureau sidekick will join me with his retirement and be my vice president."

"How do you think these franchisees will do?"

"Well, I'll be doing their advertising for them. With the notation that I'm a former FBI investigative special agent in the ad, I think they may come off as being well received in the security field."

"You said that you're a producer with a radio station, right?"

"Yes, that's me."

"How do you like what you do?"

"I've got my good and bad days just like everyone else."

Just then the phone rang. They all looked at each other. It was ten o'clock. Not that late, but not that early either. Rachel picked up the phone and said hello. She heard an orchestra playing Begin the Beguine. Then a voice said, "What do you think, Rachel? Are they great or are they great?"

"Josh? Is that you?"

"I have just formed my fifteen piece orchestra. We are now a part-time organization. You do know we will be at your service for your wedding celebration."

"And how much are you going to charge us? We cannot afford more than $2,000. In fact, we can't even afford that."

"Sweet kid sister, Rachel. You do not have to pay for our services."

"Are you kidding?" said Rachel.

"Rachel! You're my baby sister, not a customer. Besides, you have served your country for many years. I called you because I wanted you to hear us on the telephone."

"Love you, Josh, with all my heart and soul. You're the very best of brothers. I've got company here. Thank you again." She hung up.

"That was my big brother, Josh. I guess you may have heard me. Bruce, our wedding music is preordained. We have the music of Josh Ferris. They sounded so good on the telephone. I can't wait to see these guys play. A 15 piece orchestra!"

Chapter

Sixty-Two

The band was rehearsing and having the time of their lives. One of the best things about the group was that they all liked each other a lot. Josh was very happy he did the job for Bruce because he used some of that money to rent a rehearsal hall. He was getting a good price of $200 for three hours. That was a bargain. The day he called his sister he couldn't get the guys to go home. They said they would pay any extra. But there was no charge for extra time because no one was waiting to use the service. They even broke up into combos. They managed four combos out of the entire group. It would not be a stretch to say they were drunk on music.

The drummer did a solo that was like Krupa and Rich. He took his time and did flamaques big time, long single stroke rolls, rim shots, and many, many paradiddles. When drums are at solo everyone looks. They are a show all of their own. Josh was laughing so much his stomach was about to burst on him. He decided that the next time they got together he would bring his father in to listen. His musicians were not the type to have to rehearse. They were all pros. All they had to do was have a quick run before any entertainment.

Now, he had to go around and promote his newly created orchestra. The only difficulty he would have is proprietors being able to afford his group. He'd settle for 75% to begin with and after a year in would go full swing. He wanted one hundred fifty dollars per musician for a gig. That would cost $2,250 and at full promise it would be $2,815 for a little expense. His part was $500 to begin with and then go to $750,. bringing him to $2,750 and at full bloom he'd establish it at $6,375. His gigs would have to bring in a big cover charge. He was going to produce recordings and use that for sales. There were three big name places, one just a dance hall and two others that were food and dance. He had a lot of confidence in what he was doing. Proprietors would be charging at least $75 for a meal and a minimum of two drinks going for $35 a cocktail. He knew he would be a wealthy man's entertainment.

Chapter

Sixty-Three

Bruce sits in his boss's office on his last day with the Bureau. His boss isn't in the mood for Bureau business. He just wanted to spend some time with Bruce. Actually, they're talking about his new venture. It sounds like it's going to take off. They're really into it. "Bruce, I was thinking the other day about your venture. I'm not any more wealthy then other Special Agents. The Bureau pays me $12,000 more than you for my performance. If I invested in your company to the tune of, let's say $10,000, what would be my stake?"

"Now, that's a good question. I don't know that I have an answer for you, right now. I'd have to do some calculations. It could go several ways. You can lend me money for a certain period of time at, let's say, 4%. That's a lot of money during these times. If you want a stake I can give you a quarter of one percent of the profits. You would have to leave it there for seven years. So, let's say I made $70,000 gross, which brought me $56,000 net--you would get $140. But that sounds low to me. I'd give you three quarters of one percent, making it $720 a year. You can't get a big return on a small investment. However, let's say I made a million dollars. You would get $7,500. But then again, if things fell apart you'd lose your investment."

"I'm not a gambling man, Bruce, but I know you and I know you're a hustler from how you're going right now. I've got a lot of faith in you."

"Well, I sure hope it's not misplaced."

"I don't think so. If I have to lose it, I'd rather lose it to you. I'm going to send you a check for the $10,000."

"Why, I thank you for your faith in me. When you retire I'd put you on the payroll if you wanted to participate as my employee. I'd make you a vice president of something. Mike is already the vice president because of his investment."

"I didn't know he has an investment."

"Yeah, he'll drown like you if I don't make it. You could be vice president of operations, possibly. When are you hitting retirement?

"Three years from now."

"No telling where I'll be three years from now. When I get there I'll know. But one thing I'm happy about; I'll be keeping in contact with you. I was really going to miss you, but now, we'll be in touch with each other."

"Now Bruce, you have a lot of people standing in line downstairs waiting to say good-bye to you. Ninety percent of them will have tears in their eyes, including me, despite the fact we'll be in touch. I'll still miss you not being in the office. There is a big spread of goodies in your honor, like sandwiches and what goes with them, an assortment of pies and a few other foods.

I'll give you a two hour party and you can be gone. The stinkos that are responsible for your departure have sent a catalog for a gift. They're all great gifts. You'll have a hard time picking one out. The guys are waiting for you downstairs."

Chapter

Sixty-Four

The Pentagon is where the colonel's troubles began (that is, the colonel that was replaced). Like he was told, he reported to the Marine Corps Commandant.

"Colonel, what did you say to the chief?"

"Commandant, I merely wrote him a suggestion. A strategic suggestion that brought the Army into the equation."

"What made you do something like that?"

"I thought that an airdrop with service units hidden in the mountains could start a clandestine movement into learning about the business of the Taliban in Pakistan."

"Colonel! What made you think outside of the Corps?"

"Because we don't have that many paratroopers."

"You made a suggestion that was totally irresponsible. Do you know that?

You're not worth anything to the corps anymore. You will no longer be trusted to command a battalion." This brought shock to his face. His hands started to shake. "Unless you want to work at the Pentagon, it's all over for you. Do you know that? However, you'll be watched. You've cooked your goose."

The colonel sat in a chair and just about turned gray. He dropped his head onto the fingers of his right hand as he brought his hand up and showed a man that had been broken.

The commandant showed him a pitiful sigh.

"Well, Colonel. Which will it be? Are you ready to work for the Pentagon?"

"General, the Pentagon has such a bad reputation. A lieutenant colonel such as I am wouldn't even get any respect with all the generals walking about."

"Well, if you want to remain in the corps you don't have any other choice. Try it out for a while and maybe in a year or so you can decide if you want to stay or retire. That's all I have to say. This meeting is over."

The colonel got up and did the usual military moves and went out the door. The commandant moved his head from side to side, pitying the colonel.

CHAPTER
SIXTY-FIVE

Rachel got a call from mom. Mom requested her presence, along with Bruce, to show them something that had to do with their wedding. They had been busy doing things during the evenings, making arrangements for the gowns, invitations and what-not. Bruce had finally gotten around to bringing his parents to Astoria to meet his future in-laws. His siblings had not been invited because it would have been too hectic. His father and Joe took to a game of chess and were at it for a couple of hours. The women chit-chatted and had fun making plans. They were there for six hours. The Prescotts did not want to go home. They were having so much fun. They briefly met Josh and then he was gone. Yes, Mom had another little feast, different then the last one. She was a woman of variety. Bruce and Rachel couldn't stay as long as they wanted. Gee, that wedding is a time consumer.

Her high school girlfriend met another in the crowd and told her about the wedding. She got very excited. She aims to call Rachel and ask her if she'd like another bridesmaid. "We were close back in those days. I remember her telling me she was on her way to Annapolis for school. I just didn't realize it was the academy. She a big boss now."

She advised the captain she was getting married. He was elated. She advised him that she is sending him an invitation and some of the guys she used to work with. She really struck him when she advised she was marrying Bruce. The captain asked if Bruce had called her from the aircraft carrier. She advised him she bumped into him in New York and that his parents live in New Jersey. She didn't want to go into detail.

CHAPTER

SIXTY-SIX

Afghanistan with its rugged terrain and mountains, poor farming land and a misfit for a president--when we leave it will tumble again. A visitor was approaching the Cooper compound and the news was very widespread. He was coming in a jeep with feelers up front hoping to find an IED before it found him. He looked very Taliban and was securing his way through when he was held up at the last point. Marines approached him from all sides. He was not afraid. Must be something to it. "We have a suspicious person outside, sir. He wants to speak with you. He doesn't seem to have that evil attitude. We have done a thorough strip search of him and he definitely is without a weapon. We thoroughly checked his underwear, as well."

"Bring him in, Sergeant, but keep him just inside the threshold of the opening."

He comes in with a very optimistic attitude and smile.

"Thanks for seeing me, Captain. I'm grateful for that."

"State your business and your position. Make it quick."

"I look like the Taliban because it suits my purposes. They make big promises that are nothing but lies. I was born here and I will always live here. They are partly here because they are paying my people to fight with them because they know they are dirt poor and need the money. I also need the money but have avoided things that cost me money unless very basic.

I have to get my countrymen back, out of their hands. They know I'm here. They make it their business to know everything. They'll also question me about this visit. My answers to them will be I wanted to meet and speak with these people and to advise them they are a part of our problem."

"Mr. Taliban, we are a necessary force. This deployment is costing our government tens of billions of dollars. Do you think we feel at home here? We have beautiful families praying and awaiting our return."

"Please call me Abdullah. It is one of the most common names in this country. The only way to get you back home is to get rid of them. We need your input to improve our living circumstances. I am not alone. I have what you might call intelligence. That's military intelligence. I'm the head of a clandestine movement of what you would call patriots. We are believed to be insurgents ourselves. My men and one woman are extremely believable actors. We would like to work in concert with you. Do you have an encrypted phone?"

"Why do you ask?"

"I should not have bothered. I want you to know that I'm not acting now. The only way to get rid of your military is to help you rid us of the Taliban. If you are agreeable I will place an encrypted phone at your disposal on our frequency. I left the country to get this equipment. It was bought with Taliban money. There are six of us with these phones. They truly believe we are a part of them. To do this I had to take a life. They don't put all through this test, but I was one that did get tested. My people could get Academy Awards with their acting skills and that is one reason why they are so convincing. They have all sworn on the Koran their allegiance to a Taliban-free Afghanistan. We are trusted because I am a leading insurgent, myself. This is the only way to get my country back. We will transmit intelligence as to where our leaders will be for your capture. If you kill them you will get nowhere: they will just be replaced by someone else. The whole thing is to take them prisoner. Then you can question them at length. I know you think I'm lying to you. I'll just have to prove myself to get your trust. If not for Pakistan they would have no place to run. Are you willing to take the gamble and work with us?"

"As soon as I check with my superiors! It's not my decision to make."

"Before I leave I'll need several bruises from your men. I have to convince them I was mistaken about you and was mistreated. I have to show I should have known better. A couple of cuts should help convince them, just not too deep, and a punch in the face. It's got to be convincing."

CHAPTER
SIXTY-SEVEN

"You Marines have got to try harder. You have to put in more overtime. I've gotten feedback from his command. He is a Marine through in and throughout. He asked his men to be deadly with knives and guns and they were deadly with knives and guns. I have a picture that was released to me under the cover of confidential. I can't show it to you but I can describe it. One of his men became a specialist in being deadly. He threw a knife at a lookout for a group of Taliban. The knife went deep into his chest and then he threw another one into the guard's throat. He was crazy enough to take a picture, he loved what he had done so much. This is their specialty now. They are quiet killers. If it's possible, use that. It's not confidential without the photo. You can make a possible recruit feel like he is going to be one bad, very bad Marine. We have a least 50 high schools that we never went to. Call the principals and ask for permission to recruit. Don't talk about the confidential thing at the high schools. We have the demonstration platoon that is free to travel. I'll request six of them to augment your presentation. Of course, you'll have to stagger your use of them. I'll ask our commander if he would get us a car to get them around so that they can do two demos in one day."

She was getting them excited with what she was saying. She was still getting looks for her back side. It was a losing case. After all, she was a fox. She still felt the sting of being chewed out. If she continued to have difficulty with her new commanding officer she would ask for a transfer to different work in the same geographical area.

CHAPTER

SIXTY-EIGHT

Josh needed money for his group. He did the jobs for Bruce and made himself as much as ten thousand dollars. He bought a lot of music from the forties and fifties by the major himself, Glenn Miller. He also bought Harry James, Duke Ellington and Benny Goodman. He built his library into 200 tunes for which he received a discount of $500. He made several recordings for samples as he moved around exploring opportunities. He started to get jobs by breaking up the guys into combos and was successful with that. Meanwhile his name was getting around. He decided to place an ad for his orchestra by writing in the New York Times want ad section.

15 piece orchestra available for large restaurants. Sample CDs available. Call 212-339-5900 for an appointment. I'll come out to Manhattan, Brooklyn, Staten Island, Bronx and I reside in Queens. Will consider Long Island if the establishment is not out too far.

The first day his ad was out he got a phone call. It was the same restaurant owner that Bruce had installed the security system for. When he got there he was impressed with the layout. "Sir, you have a beautiful establishment here."

"Call me Jim. There's no need to be formal here. Your ad says you have a CD that I can listen to."

"I've got it right here." He handed the CD to the owner and it was placed in a hi-fi set. The owner flicked the switch and he was gone. What he did was bend his head into his fingers like he was meditating. He just stood there and listened.

"You must have the best musicians alive in the orchestra, sir."

"Hey, we're not formal here, you said. Call me Josh." "Josh, you have a sound that lights up my whole system and I'm talking my body. I could listen to your group all day. Would you accept $3,000 for a night? I have a very large clientele. Professional people. I'd have to increase their meals by possibly 7% to be able to meet your fee but I think they'll try to get to hear you guys more than once. I'm going to call my dad. He was the one that started the restaurant. He comes in once, twice a week. I added two new eating sections to it. Dad loves what I did. I'm going to get him here. He'll only be about 15 minutes. He's 83 years old and looks like he's 65. And on top of all that, he's a handsome guy with a full head of hair. My mother also looks young. Let me make that call." He took out his cell phone and speed dialed. "Dad, how are you feeling today? What, you can still take me on? You're a piece of work. Dad, I have a gentleman here that has a CD of an orchestra he has. Dad, the music is wonderful. He has a sound that is above and beyond the call of music. Come on over. I want you to hear it." He closed the cell phone. "He's on his way. He's got a Caddy SUV worth 65 grand. This restaurant has been that type of success."

Chapter

Sixty-Nine

"Here he is." His father is walking over to them. "Dad, this is Josh. It's his organization." Josh and Dad shake hands vigorously.

"It's a pleasure to meet you, sir."

"Jimmy, the name is Jimmy. No need to be formal. Let me hear that music, Jim."

Jim put the music on and Jimmy listens. His face breaks into a smile that is very wide and he shakes his head back and forth. "This music is so great, it should be illegal. My congratulations to you. Jim, do you guys have a deal yet?"

"Yeah, dad. Three grand a gig for fifteen musicians and himself."

"Jim, don't be so cheap. Music like that! Give him thirty-five hundred. Don't be a piker. Throw an extra 8% on the menu when he plays here. Josh, you're going to like this crowd. It's going to love you and your guys. Jim, word is going to get around that people should hear these guys. We're going to pick up new patrons. I can feel it. And you know I'm never wrong about business."

"Jimmy," said Josh, "I love your establishment. I've never seen a finer restaurant. You and your son Jim have the best taste there is. I'm not trying to get on your good side, either."

"Josh, you're already on our good side. When can you get started?"

"This Saturday night. Is that all right?"

"I'll have my wife here with me. We're going to be dancing."

"You're going to have a treat, Josh. My mom and dad are great dancers. Sometimes people even clear the floor for them. This may be the beginning of a beautiful friendship."

Chapter

Seventy

Captain Cooper is sitting in a group of company commanders. The commanding officer, Colonel John Windjammer, was looking at his commanders and saying, "Captain Cooper had a very odd experience yesterday. He gave me a call first thing this morning. Captain, why don't you tell them of your experience?"

"Thank you, sir. First of all I want to say it will be hard to believe and second of all where do we go with it, if anywhere at all? This kamikaze pilot of a Taliban comes up to my compound in a jeep. He advises that he wants to get rid of us so that his country can get on with a normal life. He is not really a Taliban but a patriot that the Taliban believes is among them in true spirit. He wants to get them defeated and has to work with us to do so. He desires to give us intelligence on how to defeat them wherever they may be holed up. He'll give me an encrypted phone and call in. He asked us to do a little physical damage of his person to convince the Taliban of what we did to him in his attempt to find out what kind of militaries we are. So we gave him some minor cuts and a punch very close to his eye that will turn black and blue. I must say it killed me watching his pain. So what do we do about this creature from the Black Lagoon?"

"Very well put, Cooper. What I'm thinking is my disruption over our own intelligence. Give conflicting info that will cause us confusion, from our own intelligence. One thing he can very easily do is set a trap. I say he is not to be believed. When he appears at your compound, Cooper, tell him the high command advises that he should not surrender a phone to you and tell him thank you very much but no.

Chapter
Seventy-One

Josh went home and advised his mother and father of the miracle that came about in his dealing with the Di Chiamos. He said hi to his sister, Rachel, as well.

"Hey you guys, I want you to hear what my band sounds like." He put the CD into the stereo and they all looked at him with a star-struck look.

"Josh, is that your band?" said Rachel. "Well, I'm certainly going to have one great wedding celebration. I'm breathless. My goodness, did you step in it or what! I can't wait to share this with Bruce."

"You know, Bruce has a small hand in what I have. I've done more work for him several times around. He smiles because he says I keep saving money for him. I've used his money to help get organized. I pay a small fee for rehearsals that we really don't need. However, I do it to some degree for fellowship. My guys like each other. I started breaking them up into combos and got some jobs that way. You have no idea what this father and son team, the Di Chiamos, are like. They made me feel like I blessed them. We're on for Saturday night. I can take care of your expenses so that you can be there."

"Josh," said Bruce, "we're not exactly paupers. Now, I speak for Rachel and myself and we will be paying for the night ourselves."

"And so will we," said Mom."

"We will said?" said Dad.

"You bet, Mr. Ferris. Don't try to freeload on your son. I won't hear of it."

"You guys are great. I'm so happy I might just faint. I have to make 15 phone calls now and advise my guys about Saturday night. Mom, my heart is pounding so hard."

"At least you know it's in good shape, Josh," said his mother. "I'm off to my office and headquarters. $3,500, here I come." He strutted up to his room and that was that.

"I'm so happy for him. Why do I get the feeling we're going to lose him to celebrity?"

"Mom," said Bruce, "that just might happen. But let's not think of it in a negative way. He'll buy you a new house. Wouldn't you like that?"

"I love the house I have, thank you very much."

CHAPTER

SEVENTY-TWO

Franchises for sale. The new Prescott Securities Systems Franchises was founded by Bruce Prescott, a former Special Agent of the FBI, who is putting his know-how into action with sophistication. He will be speaking at the Rutgers Solarium of practice and business quarters for the promising future of the franchises. We need security for our organizations now more than ever before. The presentation will start at 10 a.m. and last through 12 a.m. Attendance is free. Coffee, tea or juices will be served starting at 9:30 a.m. If you cannot be there send someone else in your place. You will not regret it. At this time the organization will only be accepting five applications for immediate action, with the remainder being franchised a few each sixty days apart.

Bruce's former boss was reading the ad and was elated with it. He could feel success in his bones. What he had in favor of this investment of $10,000 was that Bruce is a very tall and handsome speaker. He reeks of sophistication and is a draw himself besides what he is promoting. "I have to give him a call and advise him he's gotten me all excited."

Bruce is now going to take the gamble of moving to new quarters. He had a one year lease which has three months to go and it's inadequate. He wants to make a showcase out of it to show off the systems that he will sell and install. He is also going to hire on a part-time basis an electrical engineer to work on new systems. He wants to have at least nine systems to be available. He smiles when he thinks about Josh's much greater interest in working with him. He saves money and Josh just has the gift of installing the work. What more could he ask for? Josh, to his own surprise, wants the work to have money to work things off with his new job organization. HOT DOG.

CHAPTER

SEVENTY-THREE

Aaauugh. The Taliban was being choked to death with a wire that cut deep into his neck. The Marine that choked him had a smile on his face. *You died so nice for me. Your choking sound was like music to my ears. It was very rewarding taking you down and out. Now, I want to get another one of your brothers. I can slither around better than you can. I guess I already proved that, eh.* This Marine had no fear. He was a certified killer. He once considered being a soldier of fortune. He found out that he loved killing. This does happen in the armed forces.

The next thing he did was climb a tree and use his night glasses to search for another. He was looking as hard as an owl. He felt like he was in another world. He stayed in the tree for a bit until he saw someone. One half hour later he saw his next prey about thirty feet away. He came out of nowhere. His own troops were wondering where he was. He decided it was worth having his butt chewed out if it happened.

As he snaked around he felt so deadly. He was lit up like a Christmas tree. He really enjoyed killing these murderers. *There he is. He is on watch. Their sentry looked around without concern about any Marines really being around. He didn't realize it but the moon was right on his face. There was a group of them about 20 yards from him.* He took out his small blade and pulled his hand back as those night vision glasses held his target. Huummmmf. He threw with all he could muster in his body. There it was. Just the way he liked it. A startled look on the rag head's face. *He's wondering where it came from as he loses his breath and his body absorbs the shock of the*

*intrusion of sharp steel. He had a look about him like I can't believe this
has happened to me. He refuses to believe there is a blade sticking out
of his chest. At least the blood wasn't spurting out too much. He'll just
take out the rag he carries with him and plug up the hole as he pulls the
knife out. Then he'll crawl back to camp and they'll take care of him.*

Well, it's time for another knife. Then he pulled the larger blade
out and threw that one just a slight bit slower because his target of
the Taliban's neck was smaller. This was all done quick time. As the
guard was trying to breathe the second dagger struck the middle
of his throat. He wasn't about to deny it as he choked and gagged
and could no longer breathe. His face was now in contortions The
Marine could hear the rag head's breath struggling to breathe. He
must have been a very strong person because he shook very heavily
as he died. His eyes bulged out. He wanted to say a last few words
but that blade cut his tissue as he swallowed.

Now, he had the problem of coming down from his high.
He was sweating profusely. *America, what I have done for you
tonight was like the act of a rattlesnake. I did it for my country.
I've gotten some revenge. I have got to shut it off, now. I've turned
killer and I have to calm down. I've gone to a plateau of having
fun. Now, that's not being a Marine. You have to get back into your
Marine spirit. There is no room for killing with pleasure. Have you
no shame?* He started to head back to the other troops looking
360 degrees around him. He finally saw several of his platoon
members. The gunny crawled over to one of his men and
whispered, "Did you do anyone?" The response was, "Did I do
any one? Whatcha think I'm wearing this uniform for? I knifed
four of them that were gathered in a group. I'm bad gunny, I'm
bad. That's why I became a Marine." Then gunny said, "I'm
beginning to feel like a murderer." "Oh," said the fighter, "I'm
not killing for pleasure. My pleasure comes from knowing I
saved a lot of lives. These guys don't fight; they murder. They're
the scum of humanity the way they cut people's heads off."

"Hey we ain't killing talking here," said gunny.

CHAPTER
SEVENTY-FOUR

They were just about to start their first gig as a full orchestra. Josh was extremely happy as he was being watched by family and some friends of his band members. He hardly saw a seat that wasn't filled. The place was even bigger then he thought. There must be a hundred people in this crowd. Maybe more. He goes to the mike and makes an announcement.

"We want to thank you all for coming out this evening. It's the first day out for us and we are elated. We hope you enjoy listening as much as we enjoy playing. One thing about music--it satisfies the soul. Outside of himself, this is the greatest gift that he gave us.

So, for the first number we will play just a slightly jazzy tune called 'Intermission Riff.'"

He lifted his wand and they started in. The music was so good no one moved. The smiles were contagious. He looked at his mother and she was so happy he thought he had added ten years to her life. It was her baby that was there playing for so many people and making them smile. Her baby.

Then all of a sudden there was a couple on the floor. It was Rachel and Bruce. Wow, he didn't know his sister was such a good dancer. She made him proud. Bruce was lit up and enjoying the audience watching them. Josh was close to the end of the music and decided to add some more bars to keep them dancing. He yelled back to the coda to his musicians. They held the floor dancing until the end of Intermission Riff. They received a roaring applause. They both took a bow.

"Rachel, what a wonderful surprise! What more could a mother ask for? My son is leading a wonderful orchestra and my daughter dancing like a professional with her fiancée."

"Well Mother, I'm so glad you're so delighted. Daddy, your smile is so wide I think you have had twenty years added to your life."

"Bruce, you are going to be some husband to my daughter," said Dad.

"Daddy, we are going to have some wedding reception. I'd like to take a couple of dancing lessons. Can we?" He looked at his wife and thought, *What a smile; she's having the time of her life.*

"Anything you want, Mother. We'll compete with them."

"Did you hear that, Bruce? Dad wants to compete with us."

"However, you have to give us some points. We're so much older."

"I'll spot you 35 points. Take it or leave it, Dad," said Bruce.

"Mother, we're having a ball here tonight," said Dad.

They were all cracking up. Then Josh announced a new number.

"Ladies and Gentlemen, our next number will be 'Star Dust.' Josh hadn't noticed a gorgeous unattached brunette taking him in. She watched his every move. She had to do something to make him notice her. She actually had no escort. She was around the age of 35. She did not consider her parents to be escorts. She was the one that spotted the ad in the New York Times about the band having their initial gig at the restaurant. She was not romantically involved. She was a music teacher at one of the local four-year colleges. Her father had mentioned to her that he noticed a little sparkle in her eye. Well, then she had to punch him in the arm. He told her what a fabulous catch Josh would be. He was totally surprised when she responded "You know it." He thought to himself, *Can this be happening?* Josh was positioned so that he could see her, but was too busy to notice her.

Well, she'd have to make an effort to change that. She picked up her cocktail and stood up and stared at him. She moved slight closer to his line of sight. She stood there for several minutes. *Mr. Bandleader give me a break and check me out.*

She was really attracted to him. *I love that suit he's wearing. He'd look great in a tux.* Suddenly, he took note of her. Her smile made his heart skip a beat. *Wow, what a doll. She's going to distract me, the way she's looking at me.* His heart stated to pound. He looked back at the men. Then he snuck another look at her. She was still giving him the eye. The dress she was wearing was gorgeous. *Boy, I'd like to meet her. She's really acting like she's attracted to me.*

I'll be talking to you before you leave. I've gotten your attention, that much I know. He's trying to catch as many views of me as he can without being distracted. I'll make it my business to talk to him before we leave. I have to compliment him on his group and tell him I teach music at Hartford. I have to give him vibes to ask for my phone number. She then went back to the table. Her father looked at her with a great big smirk.

Chapter

Seventy-Five

"Got a good enough look? Did he get to see you?" said Dad. She just smiled back at him. "Don't push, Dad."

There were quite a few dancing patrons. Josh had electricity going through him. Now he slightly strained his neck to see where she had gone. The band did take notice of his change in behavior. His face was so serious in a different way. Several of them had looked in the general direction he looked in. They made faces at each other wondering what was causing him to be so distracted.

The number ended and he told them to take a fifteen minute break. They looked at each other thinking they had not started that long ago. He advised the audience that they would be back shortly.

Whoever she was, she shook him up. He went to the men's room and put some water on his face. Her father started busting her. "He takes one look at you and gives the band a break. Wow, are you that powerful?"

"He didn't take one look at me, Dad. He took several looks at me. I'll be telling him what a great band he has before I leave. I'll probably have to stand in line to do that," said his daughter.

Josh got back to the band faster than the fifteen minutes and introduced his next number as 'In the Mood' by Glenn Miller.

This lady's father asked his wife if she would like to dance. "Daddy, I'll wait for something slower."

"I'll dance with you, Dad," said his daughter.

"You will?"

"Why are you so taken aback?"

"I just didn't expect you to volunteer."

They got on the dance floor and did a modified Jitter Bug. They slowed it down. She made sure to get in his line of vision. Josh saw her and his heart jolted. She made it her business to glance at him. Their eyes met again. He thought to himself again. *I'll make it my business to see you later. You can depend on that, sweetness. You are obviously interested. That makes two of us.* He turned around and emphasized a few bars of the music. He told his lead trumpet player that he was going to take the lead on the next number that would be 'Ciri Berra Bim' by the man himself, Harry James.

---------------------------- pick up here

Josh was about to go into Mr. Performance. He got into the number after the first few bars and strutted his stuff. He stood in front of the band and serenaded. He came across as playing to her. "Kelly, he's looking straight at you while he's playing," said her dad. "You have made a connection."

"It seems to be that way, Dad."

They went back to the table after the number and his wife asked why he didn't come back to the table and take her on the dance floor. She had wanted to dance when a ballad came on. He apologized and stated that it was his daughter's fault. She admitted it was her fault. "Rose Mary, it seems there may be a connection with our Kelly and the band leader. I wouldn't have believed her if I hadn't been dancing with her. Those grandchildren we have been busting her about might just get born."

The sign said Emotional Stability rather than Psychiatrist. A psychiatrist in a war zone. Gunny sergeant Jones opened the door. There were four officers speaking to Marines. A receptionist with corporal stripes greeted him.

"Gunny, can I help you?"

"I'm looking for some input on a problem."

"I'll give you to Colonel Tucker. Just have seat over there. I'll let him know someone is waiting on him."

He came out of his office and introduced himself. "I'm Colonel Tucker. Please come into my office."

"What your name, Marine?" "I'm Gunnery Sergeant Jones." "How long have you been here?"

"Not too long sir. Arrived about six weeks ago."

"What seems to be your problem?"

"Well, I don't know if it's a problem yet. I'm just here to make sure it is a problem. Colonel, I've been doing some very real commando work. My unit is about thirty miles south of here. You can say we're a cutthroat unit. The last time I was in the field I did a job on a Taliban sentry. I sent two daggers into him. His throat, that is. Well, one to the throat and one to the chest."

"So, what I'm hearing is that you have been doing a great job. That's commendable. Now, why is that a problem?"

"Because I enjoyed it. It scared me."

"What's the difference if you're scared from him attacking you or you going after him?"

"It's not the same. I felt more like a murderer than a commando. I got joy out of it."

"So, you're worried that when you leave here you'll carry the job of killing with you?"

"Yes, that's it."

"Let me tell you, Sergeant, that back in our other wars, like WWII, Marines felt just like you do. They began to love killing the enemy. They had seen their best pals get killed and got back at the enemy for it."

"Colonel, I really haven't witnessed anyone in my company getting killed. We've brought the war to the Taliban and are cutting throats."

"Sergeant, you keep right on cutting those throats. They're taking people's heads off. They have mistreated civilians and also cut their heads off with great intimidation. Don't you feel bad about enjoying it if that happens to you. I'd love to cut one of their throats myself. What I'm going to do is write up this visit and have it forwarded to Washington for safekeeping. If you feel that you haven't left it behind go for help right away. However, in speaking to you I really don't see you having such a problem. If you have an opportunity, gun a few of them down. We just want you guys to watch out that you don't risk the lives of Afghans. We're here to teach them to handle their own war, to train their troops to protect their own country. We want out as quickly as possible. Do you leave your weapons with the enemy or make an attempt to remove them from the body?"

"It depends, sir on what the circumstances are. I actually took an unauthorized picture of one of them. It was confiscated from me with a warning that I was putting myself in danger by being distracted. They said leave the photos to the journalist."

"How many other Marines are doing the knives?" "We're all doing the knives. We're quiet and deadly."

"You know what, I hope your commanding officer sees fit to give you and the others a medal. O.K., we won't make another appointment unless you think you're coming apart."

Chapter

Seventy-Six

Sergeant Jones was back in his jeep returning to the compound. He was around three miles away and he could hear a battle taking place. He stopped the jeep on an inclining cliff to view what was going on with that small part of war. Looking with his spy glasses he saw the compound with Marines battling forty rag heads. If he could get in a little closer he could do a lot of damage. He had borrowed the deuce and a half from the supply sergeant and it had war material sitting in it just waiting to be used. He had a bazooka and dozens of grenades. They had been well hidden in the truck. He told the supply sergeant he needed it for the morning and three stripes don't usually argue with five stripes and a fabulous reputation.

He gunned the truck down the path which was supposed to be around until he came up to an embankment that would do the job par excellence. He hustled the bazookas out. A bazooka usually takes two men. Jones thought to himself, *I have to make do by myself.* He didn't know how he was going to do it but he was. He was at a high point and the battle was at a low point about twenty feet away. The spot was so good he started to salivate as to what he could do to the rag heads. This Marine played quarterback in high school and two years of college at Notre Dame, one of those years as a quarterback. He was in great shape. He took the supply of grenades and threw them at the rear of the rag heads to take out their last few men. With careful aiming he got the grenade on the last five rag heads. They didn't even know it fell on them. The blast took three of them into the air and with the remaining two that were ripped apart on the ground, he had killed five rag heads. And that was only one grenade. Uh-oh, there came that feeling again about him enjoying himself. He had a great big grin on his face. He threw another grenade and took out three of them. The Marines that were in the compound were wondering where they were getting assistance from. However, there was no time to be looking around for fear of getting hit. All they knew was the gang was losing its membership of Taliban. Jones saw just ten of them now. He took two grenades, pulled their pins and threw one right after the other. He was jumping up and down with joy. There were only three of them left. And they were in a huddle and were easy pickings. He wanted to do a lot of damage on them. He took two grenades again and threw one after the other real quick time. They never had a chance to pull back. There were twenty three or so bodies with missing limbs and also some lost their heads. Now, the action was over. He put the launcher and the rest of the grenades back into the truck and rode on down to the compound. On his way down he started blowing the horn and screaming. He rolled into the compound and jumped out of the truck.

"Well, well, well. I see you guys did some killing in my absence. Well, I have to return the truck to the supply sergeant." As he brought it in he was stared at by a few Marines. The sergeant said, "You know, most of the guys were up front in the action while we were back here taking pot shots and trying to secure our cache. You're not fooling anyone, Gunny. We saw you up there as we watched you through glasses. You were taking them down like statues at a carnival. Whether you want to admit it or not, you are a genuine hero. We're going to tell Cooper. You're going to be up for a medal."

"Don't you dare tell Cooper or I'll have to shoot you guys."

As he walked into the front part of the area the first sergeant came out and said "Gunny, hold up right there. Captain Cooper wants to see you pronto."

"Yes, sergeant." He walked in and reported to the captain. "Sgt. Jones reporting as ordered, sir."

Cooper had been staring out the window and stayed like that for a moment. He then turned around and looked at Jones.

"You know Jones, the supply guys weren't the only ones that saw you. After I got a drift on where the help was coming from I used my field glasses and saw that it was you. I could even see that smile on your face. You are the toughest hombre I have ever come across in this man's Marine Corps. I could have sworn I was looking at John Wayne, only he never had the distinction of serving his country. Now, I know you're no glory seeker. However, that's tough for you. A Marine does not do that kind of battle without getting recognition for it. You brought it upon yourself. I'm making an application for several of you tough guys. Several members of your squad got wounded beating out an army of rag heads. And there were some heroics out front. I saw a Marine yank the rifle out of a rag head's hands, turn that AK47 around and smash him so hard in the head I saw teeth fly out and a smashed skull. He also had one less eye. Not that it mattered. He wasn't going to be using that body anymore. You guys are ferocious. It's hard for me to even believe I have you under my command. I realize we're like the Special Forces. You're going in for the Distinguished Service Cross. You know that! That's one step from a Congressional Medal of Honor. First Sergeant Raymond, have our Marines fall in for a company formation and assign five men to be lookouts on the outposts."

"Yes, sir."

Chapter

Seventy-Seven

Josh advised his musicians to pack up. He was going into the office to pick up the check for the night's entertainment. He knocked on the door but no one answered. He knocked again. He just stood there getting nervous. He couldn't leave without the check. Just then Jimmy came and gave Josh a very warm handshake. "You proved tonight that I am a very good judge of character. God has seen fit to bless you with the talent to put together such a fine group. You have no idea how many compliments I have received tonight. The big question I have been asked tonight is 'is this band going to be around for a while, I hope? I told them that's up to you people. As long as you're coming to hear them there is no reason to let them go."

"Well Jimmy, I'm at a loss for words. Thank you so much for having us and telling me such a wonderful thing. You know something. I never did a lick of work tonight. I was in another world I was so happy. My mom, dad, sister and her fiancé were having such a wonderful time I almost had to cry."

"Come on in and let me give you your check. As I listened to your musicians take their solos I thought how magnificent they are. When you started playing your trumpet you sounded better than the James guy. Here you go. I can't wait for next Saturday night, already."

"Jimmy, I'm not going to sleep tonight. And thank you very much."

He didn't even look at the check and placed it in his jacket pocket. He waved good night to Jimmy. As he got back to his guys packing up he saw the lady complimenting his group. She looked at him and said "Hi I was just telling your people how great the music was tonight." She put her hand out to shake his hand. *What a doll you are. You are such a knockout.* "What's your name?"

"Kelly."

"It was very nice of you to come over and let us know how much you appreciated our music."

"Not only me, my parents as well. See them standing there? Are you going to be here next Saturday, as well?"

"From what I know I will be. Tonight was a good run to see how we would make out. The owner is extremely happy. We hope we can stay here as long as possible." The electricity was very heavy in the air between them. *What gorgeous eyes you have and such a pretty mouth.*

"Will you be here Saturday, again?"

"Oh, I forgot to tell you I teach music at a local University. I'm going to be telling my class about you. Who knows, you might get some of them to come on out. I'd say a few of them are of age to drink. If not they can drink Cokes." *My goodness, is he handsome. I don't want tonight to end. He has such curly hair. Next week I'm going to have to make a claim on you. I'm going to get you spellbound.*

As they ran out of words they momentarily just smiled at each other.

"I'll be looking for you next Saturday night, Kelly. I hope you don't disappoint me."

"Oh, I'll be here if I have to drag my parents out."

"Here comes our baby. She's glowing. We won't need any electricity tonight."

"Love, she is going to light up her own place, not ours." She came up real close to them like she had to tell them a secret. "Mom, Dad, he likes me. I can tell."

"Kelly, is that supposed to surprise us? I'd say his heart was just short of coming out of his chest."

"It had better, I thought mine was going to jump right on the floor. He is your best bet for grandchildren."

"Mother, we have got to have him over for dinner; that will cost me a good dollar. And if we have him over a second time it will be to meet your younger brothers who haven't got any girlfriends, either. Mother, what did we do wrong?"

"Nothing, Daddy. They're just anti-social."

Chapter
Seventy-Eight

Rachel had two bridesmaids. The first one convinced the other that she bumped into following her into the bridal party. They were with her mother in the living room getting invitations out.

"How many do we have all together, Mom?"

"Seventy-five considering all the lost relatives. We have some grand-nephews we're inviting, as well. We are ten weeks from your wedding, dearie."

"Ten weeks and Bruce and I will be in Europe. First we're going to Paris, then Italy and Germany."

"What! You're going to leave England out?" said a bridesmaid.

"To be honest, it doesn't faze me to see the Queen. Paris and Italy are romantic. The Brits come across as too boring. We will also go to church while we're there. We'll find a Baptist church if we don't see a Church of the Redeemer. We'll celebrate with the Lord."

"That's the attitude," said Mom. "Then he'll bless you out of your socks."

"We're going to hold off for possibly a year and a half before we start in with a family. We may only have one child. Sometimes I think I'd like to leave the Navy. Right now I have a boss I do not like one iota's worth. The captain made me feel great. He even called someone to do a job on my boss, I think. He told me I never got to him as fast as I should have. I was too delayed in reporting to him. I lost the chain of command and unfortunately was scared out of my wits with my new responsibilities. Yes, I'm admitting the big deal lieutenant commander was scared to death. I was as entitled to be scared as anyone else. What the blazes did I know about recruiting? The thought of having just about an all male organization preyed on my mind, too.

"I wonder how Captain Cooper is doing in Afghanistan. I inquired about him about a month ago. Word got to me that he was in a take the war to the Taliban and not let them come to the Marines group. They're like a commando organization. They're doing real sneaky work."

Chapter

Seventy-Nine

Bruce is in his new office with a small warehouse for all the stock he has. Now he has a full-time technician to do the installations. Mike decided to invest another five thousand dollars into the business. Mike made up his mind he was calling it quits with the Bureau in 18 more months. Bruce and the tech, at this time, were the only ones drawing a salary. The tech was getting $700 a week and Bruce decided to take a salary of a grand a week. He had to give himself the bucks for his honeymoon. He could not wait until she was his. What a knockout he was going to have for a wife. A trophy wife. Eat your hearts out, guys.

I think the love bug got to Josh. He's talking about this lady called "Kelly". He told me he would introduce her to me if she did come out again on Saturday. Well, he'd better take a picture because, at this time, one Saturday was enough for me. I'll be happy for him if he gets into a romance. He described her being about 5 ft 4 inches. A brunette with a body like Rachel. Could it be the sisters-in-law are going to be family knockouts? What about when we go out to eat together? We'll turn heads wherever we go. Ha. It's a funny thought. Bruce decided to stop the romance thinking and get back to business thinking. He had four contacts for possible franchisees. At this time he was bringing them on for $10,000 a piece. Once he got better known that would go up to $25,000. To get there he'll have to double his advertising. *It will probably take me about three years to get profitable. I'll bring Mike on for about $20,000. Between that and his pension he'll be living it up. I'll make him vice president of sales until we grow. If* *we should become very successful I'll promote him to executive vice president and fill his slot with someone else.*

It's Saturday night and they're about twenty minutes before the first musical note to be played. *Well, she's not here, yet. She'll be here. She had to pick up her parents or vice versa.* As he continues to look at the entrance she comes into view. She stands next to two guys that seem to resemble her. *They must be related. Maybe they're her brothers or cousins.* She sees him looking at her and waves her hand. He waves back. The two guys with her are very impressed. She is now entering the ballroom and her parents are pulling up the rear.

They make their way down to a longer table that they reserved, every one of them staring at Josh. His musicians are looking at them also, seeing as their boss is in another world. One musician says to the other, "Josh is gone. I can hear his heart pounding away." The other musician responds, "They are a set of bongos."

"Mom, we're going to dance before the night is out. I just met him a week ago and feel like I've known him."

Her brother Duke states, "Brother Ron, are we going to be special people to this man because Kelly is drawn to him?"

"It's always a possibility. It would be nice to have such talent in the family."

"Why don't you guys play the silent role?"

"Tsk, tsk," said Duke. "No need to be impolite to us. Now that we're here I feel more excited than before we arrived."

"That's true," said Ron. "That's true."

Josh starts making tracks toward her. Her brothers say, "Well, I'll be doggone. He's coming over to our table."

"Well, Kelly, I see you brought more family with you. I never got to meet your parents last Saturday and now I've got your brothers, I believe, as well." He put out his hand and Kelly said, "This is Ron and he is Duke. Duke isn't his real name. He picked it up as a nickname from the guys he hangs with when he's not being a loner."

As he shakes hands he says, "Well, they're good looking guys, just like you and Mr. & Mrs. …"

"My dad's name is Guy di Tempo and my mom is Glenda di Tempo, of course."

"It's is a pleasure to meet you. Mrs. Di Tempo, you are where your daughter gets her beauty from."

"Well, I think my husband also has a lot to do with that. His good looks brought me in, too."

"Well, now if you'll excuse me, we're going to start making music. Kelly, I'm going to stop by after we're into playing for a while and I'd like to dance with you, if I may."

"I'd love to, Josh."

"Of course you know they'll be staring at you considering you'll be dancing with me. Now, the next time you come, if your brothers accompany you, it would be nice to see them with some ladies. What do you say to that, guys?"

They looked at each other and hunched their shoulders. "I'm sorry to say the cost of the evening would be on the difficult side for me."

"Think nothing of it, bro. I'll subsidize you. I believe we'll both have ladies with us. And we would love to have you meet them."

"That's a deal. I'll make it my business to come by and personally introduce myself to them." Then Josh winks and they all have a laugh.

Duke says, "Kelly, I really like him. How about you, Ron?"

"I like him very much. Kelly, you're going to have to marry him."

"Amen," said her father. And then her mother repeated it.

Chapter

Eighty

Special Agent Micky Smith, Bruce's old boss, is reading the papers and sees a little change in Bruce's ad for franchisees. *I think I'll get him on the phone if he's available.* He dials and thumps on his desk top. The phone rings just twice and Bruce picks up. "Prescott Security Systems, Bruce Prescott speaking."

"Bruce, it's Micky Smith. How goes the business?"

"It's good to hear from you, Micky. It's going better than I anticipated. I've hired a full-time tech and he has installed eight systems and works the phone in between. I like him big time. He's working a full-time schedule. I've lined up four franchisees and I'm going to Texas and California to sign them up. Since they're in the early part of the business I'm only charging them $10,000 for a franchise. Of course, then I'm getting a 20% profit on all the parts. I'll bring the first batch with me since it will not be that much if any and they'll buy the parts from my supplier that will send me my part."

"I agree with you. I can't believe how successful you are, already."

"Well, I've spoken in a very business type manner with a very positive glow to it. I have to get them excited, to want to come aboard. Then when I make the contract with them, being tall, rugged looking and a handsome devil, they want to be a part of my act."

"Bruce, you are too funny. Would you still take me aboard for a staff officer? You know, a vice president of a department."

"Would you relocate, Mick?"

"Where would you have in mind?"

"Oh, I don't know, possibly Florida or California. You would become a branch of the business and build it up there getting franchisees. Then I wouldn't have to travel as much."

"It's a thought. We have time to go. Of course I may not retire for another five years."

"Mick, we'll play it by ear.'

"Nice talking to you, Bruce."

CHAPTER
EIGHTY-ONE

The company was in formation and the battalion commander was facing the Marines, along with Captain Cooper. The captain speaking to his men had told them that they were a company of extremely brave men. They were the kind of men that their country could be extremely proud of. They were going to be written up in the local newspapers and the Navy Times. He then took a list of medals and the men receiving them. He began to shout, "Gunny Sergeant Jones will be awarded the Navy Cross for heroic activity in which he took advantage of a strategic point of ground and was destroying a multitude of enemy fighters that were attacking his fellow Marines, Sergeant Morris will be awarded the Navy Distinguished Service Medal as he stood his ground and killed five enemy terrorists. Corporal Steiner, Corporal McGinness, Lance Corporal Jacoby and Lance Corporal Di Giovanni will be awarded the Silver Star for bravery in going into hand to hand combat and killing twenty enemy terrorists. Sergeant Josiah will be awarded the Bronze Star supporting the actions of his fellow Marines.

"Presenting and affixing these awards will be Colonel Stanford, our battalion commander, who has notified personally the families of these Marines." The Captain did an about-face and saluted his commanding officer, taking a position where the colonel had stood as the colonel went to each Marine, pinned the medal on their chests, shook hands and congratulated each one of them. These men had tears in their eyes throughout the ceremony, demonstrating the pride that they felt as members of the United States Marines.

Chapter

Eighty-Two

Josh and Kelly danced on the last dance and the crowd, seeing that he had gone to bring Kelly to the floor, elevated her stature as to being someone very special to the orchestra leader. Her parents and brothers were beaming from ear to ear.

As they danced they were being applauded because they had never danced with each other before and were doing it so gracefully. They were carrying on conversation and the audience was carrying on conversation, as well.

"They are a beautiful couple, aren't they?" says a lady. One gentleman said, "They seem like they are going to become an item. A woman stated that she had done well for herself dancing and finding favor with such a handsome and talented man.

Kelly said, "I can imagine what they're all saying to each other."

"That you are a beautiful woman. Can I pick you up one evening and take you to dinner?"

"I would say that would be a lovely evening. How about Friday night?"

CHAPTER
EIGHTY-THREE

The battalion was on alert to use night vision and look for the rag heads planting roadside bombs in commando style. They had to travel quietly and then leave their vehicles. Hit the dirt and crawl, listening with special air phones for voices and activity. They had no idea how long they would have to crawl and went into what they considered territory the Taliban would do the dirty work. They were as low as humans can get in camouflaging. They even used body waste to keep the IEDs people-free.

"I'm getting traffic now. It's picking up as I move farther." A corporal was doing the monitoring. "Captain, we are onto something here."

"This is the captain speaking. I want you all to spread out as we go forward. There is some small light coming into view." As they moved in they heard them talking. "O.K. men, let's close in on them. I don't want to kill them. I want them for prisoners and try to get them to talk."

All of a sudden the rag heads thought they heard something and became apprehensive. They realized they were too late in noticing as they became surrounded. One pulled out a knife and was looking to see who he could kill and ended falling down and moaning with a knife in his back. There were six of them and they were carrying twelve IEDs. "Well, well," said Cooper. "We probably saved at least two of our Marines. Who is the leader here?" he asked. No one answered. Well, we can take care of that. Doolittle, ask them who is their leader in Pushtin.

A Taliban tribesman said, "No need to speak in Pushtin. I am the leader here. You'll find that I'm quite stubborn to give you the information you're looking for." Well Mr. leader I know something about being stubborn myself. As of this moment you're my prisoners. We're taking you back with us."

"Considering you outnumber us, Mr. United States, we have no choice but to go with you. This will be temporary. After all, we are excellent fighters."

"Strip them of their weapons. Make sure you search them thoroughly for knives. They're all a bunch of cutthroats. They specialize in cutting heads off." As one of them gave resistance to a Marine the Marine hit him so hard he broke his nose and then continued to beat him, letting out his anger. The captain didn't try to put a stop to it. The rag head was yelling, "You broke my nose" in Pushtin. The Marine said, "I broke your nose. I'm so sorry. Would you forgive me, Mr. Taliban? Now get a move on," as he shoved the rag head. The leader said, "We will avenge you. I will try to make it my business to get a knife and do some cutting Marines, or are you Army?

That remark got another Marine very angry. He came alongside the leader smacked him in the back with the broad side of his weapon. As the leader jerked his head back he punched him with all the strength he could muster and punched him in the ear. Their leader screamed out in a great deal of pain. Then he yelled out again. "We will avenge you, you American scum." Gunny came up behind him and threw his wire around his neck and asked one of the Marines to take an end. As they pulled the blood flowed as it cut in by an inch and as the body fell Gunny cracked his skull open. And then he said,

"Now we don't have to hear from him anymore. He had some tongue in his mouth." He looked around and the insurgents looked away, their faces full of fear. "You don't like it when it's on your side of the fence, do you? You're not even human. You cut off heads to amuse yourselves."

A half hour later they came upon their vehicles and loaded them into the trucks. They were starting to really mistreat them and Cooper did not care one hoot. The heck with regulations. They don't abide by any rules of decency; why should we?

Chapter
Eighty-Four

They were now at the Church of the Redeemer in Astoria, Queens. They were minutes away from the ceremony. Dad and Rachel were talking to each other.

"Dad, I am so nervous!"

"Well sweetheart, I can tell you, you don't have a corner on it. I've got castanets between my knees." Rachel cracked up.

They music started and they looked at each other. They were coached to move out. They took small steps, small and slow. The church that holds 3,000 believers had a hundred people at the wedding. As they made their way up the aisle her father rubbed his thumb on her hand to try and keep her calm. He whispered to her, *I'm glad I only have one daughter.*

Bruce was watching with his older kid brother as his best man standing next to him. As Rachel came into sight he said to himself, *I can't believe I'm finally going to marry her. I'm so happy. Rachel is going to be mine, at last. I don't have to hope any more. I've come a long way since meeting her at Annapolis. What a lucky day that was.*

Her bridesmaids were very beautiful women as well. They were wearing red gowns with a chemise body to the gown. Rachel wore a silvery gown with fancy twists and a trailer with two second cousins holding the trailer. Yes, they went all out. As they approached the pastor Bruce moved in next to her. A man could not possibly be happier.

The nuptials were very emotional for them. Bruce held her hand like it was a precious stone. They smiled at each other.

When the pastor told Bruce he could kiss the bride, he went into a deep kiss. He held it and enjoyed it. She had to pull back from him. The pastor then had them face the congregation and announced, "Ladies and Gentlemen, I give you Mr. & Mrs. Bruce Prescott."

CHAPTER

EIGHTY-FIVE

The photographer was taking their picture as they came out of the church building. They were going to have a part of their photo session at this point. They had all kinds of confetti thrown at them. Josh's group was saturating the sidewalk. They had purchased a very large bag and made sure every last one had made its faith.

They made their way to the banquet hall, which is where the orchestra was performing. There was a big discount on the room rental and a slight discount on the food. Hey, Jim and Jimmy had to make a buck, too.

We had pictures taken with Mom, Dad and Josh; with Mom and Dad alone; with Josh alone; And then with his parents, and his siblings. We also went back to the church, where we took more pictures. The photographer was a band member and he was getting just a five percent profit. These guys were saving a bundle on things that were very costly.

Then Rachel called her former boss, from Annapolis Naval Academy, and took a photo with him. "Rachel, you have no idea how much I have missed you. I was even at the point of regretting getting you that promotion. I was going to retire and made one last entry for admiral and was recently advised that I could get a star within three months."

"You're getting a star and I'm now married. What a joyous day for myself and you're getting a wonderful future. My father likes you big time. Did you know that? He told me so last night. You know what else he told me? He hopes you invite him to Annapolis and give him a grand tour."

"Your dad wants to come down? We're both on the same wave length. I had it in mind to invite him. Between the two of us we can start a ruckus. My wife had a great deal of fun with your mother, as well. I'd love us to become friends. That would keep me closer to you."

"Now you're going to make me cry. Remember when you handed me my new shoulder rank and told me I was out of uniform, going from lieutenant to lieutenant commander? I almost broke out crying."

"I'll never forget that as long as I live. I love you just like a daughter. There is a possibility you may see more of me now."

"I would love that."

"You know something that bothered me today?" said the captain.

"What was that?"

"Your husband has got to be the commander that was assigned to work at the registrar's office about just over a year ago. If it isn't him he has a twin brother he doesn't know about," said the captain "It's him, Captain. He came knocking at my door when I first arrived." During this photo session, which was supposed to be only one shot with her former boss, she signaled the photographer to take a couple of more so that they could converse in private.

"That's when he had the nerve to want to give me an engagement ring. He said he was not at liberty to discuss being at the school. I turned him down big time. Then I gave in to going to dinner with him because I had skipped a meal."

The photographer had shown that what he took was quite enough.

"Captain, I'll see you later." He bowed to her as he moved backwards. He then went to his wife as she made the remark, "I can see the love in your eyes for her as though she was born to you, Oscar."

"It shows that much, Mother? You know something. Her parents and we are going to have a lot of fun together. I'll be seeing her again through them. Today is a glorious day, sweetheart."

Chapter

Eighty-Six

"Captain Cooper. I have spoken on your behalf to General Lakewater, who is in charge of our division. The work your men and you have done out here is just the opposite of what was going on before you came. Your men have been absolutely deadly. I'm putting you up for a silver star, not for heroics but for outstanding leadership. So, Captain Cooper I shot myself in the foot. Now, they want you to return regardless of the fact that you've been here such a short time and are being placed as commander of a new company. Your company will be made up of recruited and veteran Marines. You'll have a special forces type command. They'll be clandestine wherever they go. You've been in the Corps. for only three years. How did you obtain the rank of captain so fast?"

"Quite simply, sir, there was a need for a new company commander. I was a leading candidate and so they cut my time in grade to suit their needs. You know what I predict?"

"What's that, sir?"

"You'll make major before others make captain with the same longevity you have. They're going to go big on what you might call the 'quiet death' It saves American lives. We want to meet the enemy where he lives and we want to do it quietly. You'll be training Marines to become experts in what what they call the 'the dagger theory.' They will reward these Marines with a type of infantryman's badge like the Army awards. It will be in red and look somewhat similar to the bayonet but not the bayonet. It will probably have a blade designed like a serrated edge. This weapon will be a specialty of its own. You're going to leave within twenty four hours. Say good-bye to your troops. You'll take a helicopter out of here at seven p.m. tomorrow. I won't see you again, Captain. Go with God."

Chapter

Eighty-Seven

Bruce went and sat a few with his old boss Micky Smith and Mike.

"You are one lucky hombre, Bruce. You have a trophy wife; you know that don't you?" said Mike.

"You would have to say that, Mike. I don't know if you remember or not but you happen to have a very attractive wife, yourself."

"Yes, yes, I do. But I've been married for twenty-five years and I don't think about it that way. What about you, Micky?"

"I've been married 32 years and I feel I have a beautiful wife, as well. But she's not going to turn heads like Rachel does."

"Aw come on, guys. Give me a break. It took me one second to want to grab her and kiss her on the spot when I bumped into her at Annapolis. I'd probably still be single if I hadn't gone on that assignment. Justin sent me on it just to get rid of me. He never had any use for me as an agent and I didn't give any reason to dislike me."

"Yeah, you did." said Mike.

"Oh yeah, what?"

"He thought you were conceited because you're tall and handsome."

"Well, it can't be helped. The women never give it a rest. Maybe that's why I'm a humorous person. I take the edge off that way."

"Bruce, your spread of foods is so delectable. Lookie here, our wives are in a B.S. session with Rachel."

"Come to think of it, I want to get together with you guys some day. I'd like to have a barbeque with ya. What do you say to that?"

"That's great, Bruce. I'm up for it. How about you, Micky?"

"You're darn tootin. Glad you asked."

The orchestra was filing in. And you wouldn't believe it, but Josh asked Rachel if it would be all right for Kelly to come. She wanted to meet Rachel. She's there filling a chair with the band.

"What! Another looker. How did Josh get her?"

"Well guys, let me tell you something. Josh is like me. Tall and handsome. She went after him. She's got him all shook up. I have to say, I think Josh is gone. He has no defense against her and I don't believe he wants one, either. He told me he was going to take her out for dinner and changed his mind. He had her come here, and as I said, at her request. He had told her his sister was getting married."

"Bruce, let's have a four-family barbeque. He'll be just about married to her about that time."

"Gee, guys, why don't we rent a hall and have a banquet?"

"Because then Mom is going to want in, too."

The guys all cracked up. They thought that was a riot.

"I'll see you guys. My trophy wife and I are going to be dancing in a bit while everyone watches us. My brother, the best man, is about to make the announcement. I don't know why I didn't ask Mike to be my best man. Why do we have to go for family instead? My brothers call me the cop." Mike and Micky went into an uproar.

The music started and Bruce put his arms around his fox. "Baby, let's show them how to dance. I can't wait until I have you alone."

"What do you think I keep thinking about? Just the two of Us, grabbing our flight to Hawaii in two more hours."

"Do you think we can consummate our marriage on the plane?"

"You devil you, Bruce!"

"I'm game if you are. Technically, we aren't Mr. & Mrs. until that happens. And since we're married we are not committing a sin."

"Rachel, I'm not going to last more than five minutes, tops. The excitement is just going to be too much."

"Well, I agree with you, my dear husband. You're not going to last five minutes. Gee, I'm glad no one knows what we're talking about. We're dirty old people already."

The music started with one of the most beautiful marriage songs, 'My Romance'. So it's not really a marriage song. They already had fancy foot work. Bruce, at times, watched on television the dance competition. So he was a great leader and she was a great follower. The crowd of one hundred and fifty-one (now including Kelly) had applauded for quite some time. After a decent amount of time Mom and Dad joined in and they got applause as well.

All the guests that never heard the group before were mesmerized by their beautiful sound. Watching Josh, her brother, leading the orchestra created a stir. Is that Josh's band? My, how good they are. Then Josh took his trumpet and started to take the lead, and doing a lot of ad libbing, sounded so good he was applauded time and time again. A better wedding reception could not be had.

Chapter
EIGHTY-EIGHT

Captain Cooper was on a transport plane looking at other Marines on his way back to the states. He felt a lot of heartache as he looked at the damage to the troops. This was sort of an overflow of men and women that didn't make the regular medical transport. They were headed for Walter Reed Medical Center. He was going to take another military passenger plane back to his unit. He was hoping they would not fuss about his return to start up this new unit. He was to be commanding a detachment to the 5th Marines. He was going to put an ad in the Navy Times mentioning his new command and the want of a unit of 40 Marines to be dispatched to clandestine locations as a unit or possibly only a part of the detachment.

On his way he thought he might stop off at Annapolis Naval Academy to see if they might have changed their attitude toward him. He had left in a bad manner because he had been on the weed. However, he and several buddies were intimidated into the purchases because of the greed of a superior officer. This was also done at West Point Military Academy. He was hoping to salvage his reputation.

The plane landed at the nearest air force base to Walter Reed and they all, with the exception of himself, took transportation to the hospital. He didn't want to go straight to his unit. He needed to go to Annapolis. So instead of taking a military flight he decided to spend his own money to fly to his unit and make this visit.

He found himself looking at Annapolis one hour later. It was nine a.m. when he went to the mess hall and sat down for breakfast. He was stared at because he wasn't a part of their organization, a stranger at the academy. He took a seat where the officers sit and went at his breakfast. He looked around the cafeteria and had flashbacks to his days as a midshipman.

In his thoughts someone had mentioned his name out loud.

"Cooper, is that you?"

He looked at this lieutenant and was at first puzzled and then he recognized him.

"Hello Smith. You are looking good. What unit are you with?"

"I'm working on my masters and teaching."

"You know your photo was not in the Navy Times; however, your name was. I had a hard time believing you were the same pal I had here. I wasn't the closes of buddies but I knew you pretty good. You are a new man. You left in a dark shadow and have become a hero of sorts. They expedited you to a captain and sent you to the big bad land where you were said to be a commando org."

"You know Smith, as I read it, myself. I thought they were talking about a different person. I felt that I had made up for my reputation here with my two pals."

"Now you are on your way back?"

"Yes, the Corps has fallen in love with me. I'm a dangerous person. I'm commanding a special unit. You have what about two years before you're eligible for captain?"

"Yes, that's about right."

"If I could pull it off would you like to join my unit? Nah, I don't think you're its type. Then again, you won't be training.I was going to offer you a chance to be my exec."

"Thanks for the thought and I apologize for not speaking to you as a subordinate. It's that you surprised me."

"Perish the thought, Smith. I'm not a glory hound. I'm going to see if I can see the commandant."

"He's not here anymore. You just missed him. He transferred out just last week."

"I'd say hello to some of the instructors; however, I diverted myself and I have to get going. Coming here I now have to pay for flight back to my unit.'

"Captain Cooper, it was a treat seeing you and I commend you for what you have done and what you are going to do.

"Well thank you, Smith."

CHAPTER

EIGHTY-NINE

He arrived at 2 p.m. and reported to the battalion commander. Colonel Scott was happy to see him. He stated that he was going to be watching his unit only because he loved what they were going to be about.

"Cooper, I am very happy to have you aboard. I'm happy-go-lucky about your assignment here. I'm anxious to watch your men train. That will fascinate me. Your record at the big place is outstanding. The label for your compound is Scott Detachment. Your troops are waiting for your invite. I'm giving you permission to pick your own men. This is your specialty and you know what's best. I have a list of 60 men. You'll have to call them and see who you want. Fly them in, if necessary; however, keep the budget in mind."

"Yes, my first choice is Gunnery Sgt. Jones. He was training Marines, himself. He reported to the dismissed commander."

"Dismissed, what do you by dismissed?"

"I cannot clarify it, sir. I had no idea why. His time there was short. His replacement didn't see the need to make him in charge of a unit that reported to him. He is deadly and I will ask for his transfer, on that basis. He has the expertise. I'm sure some vets out there have his expertise, as well."

"Go with it, Captain. Give me an invite now and then. This group is too important for me to constantly look over your shoulder."

CHAPTER

NINETY

"Rachel, I'm glad I don't fly. The airport process is nothing short of a nightmare. It's too bad it's a necessity. I don't look forward to the second round. Where do you want to go today?"

"Nowhere. Let's just lie on the beach and have great meals. Except that I would like to see the Crowd of Seven. Their reputation is unreal. They have been all around the world. Their impersonations are without equal. One of my bridesmaids told me about them. She advised not to miss them. We can catch them at seven in this very hotel."

"Now I'm twice as excited as I was."

He started hugging her and the passion started to flow. She was really letting loose, not being reserved as she always is. "Bruce, you take my breath away. I never let you know that before because I didn't want to have a fat head on my hands. It's in your family blood. All your siblings are attractive people. You are the oldest and the cop of the family."

"I thought we came here to have a fantastic time. Leave my siblings where they are. Whatever state they live in. My brothers also wanted to be cops. They just won't admit it. At least they have a lot more money than I have. The turkeys. They're only doctors because my father gave them a lot of spending money if they became doctors."

"I'm sorry I brought them up. I was referring to good looks. I didn't ask for their histories."

"Well, one thing leads to another. The turkeys."

"Let's do our favorite pastime. That is, outside of the other favorite pastime. Let's have a great lunch."

"Why, you're a dirty old lady already."

"There are no dirty old ladies, Bruce. There are only dirty old men."

Chapter

Ninety-One

Mike was sitting in the office of Prescott Security Systems. He had been in the new office just once and was now putting more organization into it while Bruce was living it up in Hawaii. They had received a new shipment of parts and he was putting it away. One thing about Bruce. He was not cutting any corners. The stock was the best. Mike had received the messages left from potential franchisees. The recession became an instrument of people attempting to go into business for themselves. There were five of them inquiring about joining the franchise. Mike thought that Bruce had a stroke of genius when he decided to go in this direction because of the handwriting on the wall about losing his job. The business was growing on nearly a daily basis. Their technician was setting up two systems a week. Their total installation up to that day was twenty-five customers and counting. They received upgraded jobs, giving their organizations an upgrade. Bruce had impressed them into tearing out their present systems when he showed them what they weren't protecting. These new customers were very impressed. Bruce had no idea he was going to be such a good salesman. Mike had to be returning these calls. What he was doing was making calls outside the office at lunch time and advising these potential customers to call him back in the evening because he was running overtime. When they called he took all the information and advised that they would be contacted in roughly two weeks. This was the best he could do to cover for Bruce while he was romping around. Mike also had dollar signs in his eyes. He was an executive officer of this enterprise. He wasn't doing a menial part-time job.

Chapter

Ninety-Two

"I called my mom and dad to let them know I was thinking about them and having a wonderful time, as well. Are you going to do that for your parents?"

"Well, since you just sent me on a guilt trip I have to. I just don't want my parents to pass away because I never call. I also don't want my brothers or brother to be there and then I have to talk with one of them."

"Bruce, you have to stop being like that with them. So they call you a cop, so what! Besides, I like them. I want to see more of them. That goes for your sisters as well."

"Well, listen to you. If I had known you would be thinking like that I may have reconsidered joining up with you."

"Are you kidding me? You sighed when the ceremony was over with. You were deliriously happy. You finally had me for yourself. Now listen to you. You nincompoop."

"You really know how to hurt a guy. You're right. I do have to change my attitude. But to do that I think you need to talk with my bros. I think you have to tell them to give me a break."

"I'd have no problem doing that. They can't talk with me without a twinkle in their eye. They're lucky their wives don't see it. I'll have them wrapped around my finger just like I have you."

"Oh, is that so?"

Bruce went and wrapped his arms around her bobbing her around and dumping her on the bed. Then he jumped on the bed too and started kissing her. After the first kiss they decided it tasted good and went for the second, third and many more to follow. Excitement was beginning to be the name of the game. They decided to roll the covers down and indulge for a nice long while. Bruce asked if they should make a baby and Rachel said, "Let's wait a year or so. In the meantime we'll get a lot of practice."

Chapter
Ninety-Three

"Daddy, Rachel called from Hawaii and they're having a fabulous time. She even got Bruce to call his parents. You do know that's hard for him to do. She advised me she is going to make him change his attitude toward his brothers. Quite frankly, I didn't know he had an attitude toward his brothers. She said they have put in a lot of beach time. They'll be home the day after tomorrow. She said she had a couple of surprises for me. Now I can't wait until they get home."

"Nothing for me?"

"I suppose so. She just didn't say. I know she'll have something for you and Josh as well. Josh's music made her wedding reception such an enjoyable night. Speaking of Josh, I think he's a goner. Kelly is beautiful, just like Rachel. I think it's all over for Josh. She melts him, in case you haven't noticed."

"I've noticed all too well. She melts me too."

"Now Daddy, we're not talking about you. She's got no business melting you. That's my job and don't you forget it."

"Sorry I said anything, Mother!"

Chapter
Ninety-Four

Cooper went up to see the commander. He asked the first sergeant if he could manage a few minutes with the colonel. He was in a very nice orderly room as the company clerk was typing away on forms. The clerk was a very chubby corporal and was doing a job on a sandwich with the clock saying only nine in the a.m.

"Absolutely Captain. No problem. Just let me knock on his door and advise him you'd like a minute or two."

The sergeant took a bit of time and returned. "Sorry it took so long, sir. He was just ending a phone call. He's waiting for you now."

"Thank you, sergeant," said the colonel.

"Well, well, if it isn't the commando commander. What's up?"

"Sir, I just had a big disappointment."

"How's that?"

"Gunnery Sergeant Jones would love to come over. His commanding officer has a hold on it. He advised he could transfer out but he'd have to wait a bit. He said the old man, even though he's only a company commander, wants him to do some more killing before he leaves. How about that!"

"I find that hysterical. I can't wait to meet him. That's a riot. Have you contacted others?"

"Yes. I have five veterans coming. They're transferring as we speak. They had the audacity to salivate while speaking on the phone with me. They nearly scared me."

"Captain, you keep talking like that and I'm going to consider you a standup comic. You should have seen your expression. No one says you can't have any fun just because you wear an armed forces uniform. Have you got the necessary tools to hone your guys on?"

"I'll have the last of them tomorrow. I ordered five poles as round as a throat without the Adam's apple." He cracked the colonel up again.

Chapter
Ninety-Five

"Well, we had a fabulous time, love."

"I got Mom all excited telling her I had a couple of things for her. I didn't tell her I had a couple of things for Dad. Josh is getting a nice looking net and boat to go with it. Speaking of Josh, Mom says I have a new sister-in-law coming up quick time. She says the members of his band are getting a kick out of him. He's actually only taken her out once. She didn't count our wedding reception. I like the fact that she has a degree in music. You know she teaches at a local school, I think a university. I look forward to a good relationship with her. I wonder how Captain Cooper is doing in Afghanistan? He's a top-notch Marine. The best of the best. Out of curiosity I'd like to contact him. I don't know if it will be easy or hard to get through to him if I do at all."

"Well, you'll be finding out. I hope things have gone smoothly with Mike. I told him to put stock away and return phone calls as they came in. I asked him to tell the people to expect a call in the evening. I don't want him calling on Bureau time. I'll just reimburse him for the calls. So when are we coming back to Hawaii?"

"I don't think next year would be too soon. The wonderful aroma of Hawaii gets to you."

Chapter
Ninety-Six

"We are going to be a nightmare to terrorists. They are going to wish they decided to do otherwise. We are going to train in hand to hand combat and Ju-Jitsu when in close contact. If there is to be any close contact. However, fighting isn't want we want to do. Just killing. We want to either strangle by a sharp wire, cut throats or impale them with knives. The most popular of these methods is the dual knife act: One blade for the chest that goes to the heart which we know is really centered and the other blade goes to the throat. If you hit the heart they'll go down ka-boom. Real quick. Then you won't need the second blade. If they're trying as hard as they can to stand you whiz one over for the throat. Only recover your weapons if you can do so safely. We'll keep a supply of blades other Marines don't. It would be to your advantage to sharpen your weapon every night. It makes the kill go better. The blade comes out faster and you protect yourself faster.

"Sometimes we may split up and go to several places. Mostly I hope to do our job together. Now, recently, Christmas brought us bad news. We almost lost another plane in one of our cities. The terrorist was trained in Yemen. They say Yemen has quite a population of those training there. I'd like go to Yemen with a large force. However, we can't just go there and invade them. We also have to look like them. I've acquired a tanning instrument. Anyone trying to use it for self gratification can count on being court martialed. I hope I am clear on that. We have to darken ourselves as best we can. I've also brought in several Marines that speak the dialects that most Arabs use. You will learn to speak the language as best as you can. Remember, your life depends on how well you learn it. That includes writing it. We're going to be a busy detachment. From time to time Colonel Windjammer will drop in on us. He is a big fan of our type of warfare. He is glad to have us in his organization. I'd like to go up to 100 strong or more. Getting into Yemen, in our own style, will take a few months. Other Marines will be there and we have to be careful not to give ourselves away or get into a fight with another Marine."

CHAPTER
NINETY-SEVEN

"Well, we're home, dear, and we have to see what we're going to do for housing in the sense that I'll have to stay at your place for as long as possible. However, that will have to be just for sleeping. I'll have to have calls forwarded to your place. Your place is good enough for a while. Having my place sort of complicates things. I do know that you will not be authorized to sleep there. It's strictly for military personnel."

"There's no problem, love. My apartment isn't that small. I have three rooms. The living room is good square footage. I can't believe we didn't talk about this much. That's because I didn't think it a big deal. My job with the Bureau gave me a decent paycheck after my promotion that didn't last long."

"Well, let's take a nap. You can check up on Mike tomorrow, go out to eat and take the souvenirs over to Mom and Dad. They're going to act like big kids. I'll love that. They're so precious to me."

"And me as well. They are my parents-in-law and I love them very dearly. They do have a new son, you know. I have several more people to love me now. So there!"

"Bruce, sometimes you're just too much. I have more people to love me now just like you do. Only I have more of them. So there."

They cracked up and hugged each other. He looked into her eyes and smiled while bending for a long winded kiss.

"What do you say to some sexual exercise before we take a nap?"

"I was just thinking the same thing. That's a perfect suggestion."

Chapter

Ninety-Eight

"Mr. Phelps? I'm Mr. Connors. I'm returning your call for the franchise with Prescott Securities System. How are you today? I know you must have a lot of questions. What I'm going to do is e-mail you questions and answers. If you can't find your answer from it you can call me back and we'll answer your question then.

"It is in your favor to join this franchise now while it's cheaper. Some time down the road it will probably double in price. The business is very young. It's under a year old and has had a great deal of success already.

"Have you ever been in a franchise before? No. Well, by all indications, you may have it for a very long time. We have the highest quality elements for our systems. Our own business has surprised us. Being Mr. Prescott is a former agent, he is much more thorough in his vision of what the best system calls for.

"I'm going to get your Q and A out for you right now. As I said, you can get your answer quickly if it is not in our e-mail. You take care now."

CHAPTER

Ninety-Nine

The lights from the headlights went shining through the front windows of the living room. Mother is very excited. She feels like a kid and Dad is right there, also feeling like a kid. They're watching them walk over to the door and are about to ring the bell. Mom opens the door and yells, "Rachel!"

"Hi Mom. How are you doing? Daddy, how are you? Well, as I said, we have some souvenirs for you."

"Well, come on in before Daddy whittles in his pants."

"Thanks love, I appreciate that."

"Did you hear what she said, Bruce? How embarrassing." Bruce and Dad shook hands as Dad was all smiles.

"Had a good time, huh? I still remember mine. That's when she used to be all over me." Then he winked and said, "Still all over me!"

"Now Daddy," said Mom. "Let's not go there."

It took an hour and a half before they stopped talking about the gifts. Now Mom had everyone in the kitchen making Bruce salivate with all the goodies. He could always count on salivating over at Mom's. She had him thoroughly spoiled and loved every minute of it. She considered him the perfect son-in-law. A very proper person. Not to mention how handsome he was. *These guys are going to make some beautiful kids for me to play with.*

CHAPTER
ONE HUNDRED

Twenty five Marines were snuck into Yemen. They traveled by submarine and then were rowed under cover of darkness. A force of Marines before them built a layout that was housed in a mountain with heavy doses of weeds and branches inlaid into a very large door. They fit in very comfortably. They looked like rag heads themselves. They were speaking basic Arabic. What they were was Marines turned actors, the best of actors since their lives depended on their ability to pull it off. They had six months of training and were eager to initiate it. They came in five boats before the sun would rise. It was so dark they bumped into each other. The theme of their entry was silence. Nothing was said above a whisper. Cooper went along to make sure all went the way he had intended but returned to his company compound where there were twenty-five others still in training. They were using encrypted transmission. They first had to learn the lay of the land to be able to function as efficiently as possible.

As a reward for their going into this clandestine effort Cooper had every one of them promoted up a grade. The lowest ranking man was a Corporal. They had an abundance of supplies hidden with them. But they walked around from three in the afternoon looking like any other citizens of the country. There was absolutely no reaction from the natives. They all went to different stores to make purchases. They had to buy things to make themselves look active. However, they were on a far end of a mountain. Their code word was open sesame. They even had showers and a latrine above water to be disposed by nature.

After being settled down for a week it was now time to strike. They didn't work in full force. They had three-man teams to watch each other's backs. They had a first lieutenant commanding them. There were eight teams. The biggest sport was sharpening their knives. They did say they would be happy to shave. Most of them hated wearing a beard.

CHAPTER

ONE HUNDRED ONE

They picked up on where the Taliban and Al Qaeda were because they were asked to join up with them. Several of them did pretend to sign up with them. Being in the group gave them cover. However, once they killed they immediately went back to their hideout or just went there until they could ship out. They didn't want to bring suspicion to themselves. The insurgents had no idea they had death joining their ranks. Once in a group, if they did get into one, they tried very hard to take out three of them. They gave themselves a busy night.

They would go up to a sentry and pretend conversation with a brutish movement to snap a neck or a very quick move to sink a knife into their backs with a twist. They stood around in the late evening hoping to be asked to join up and tried to pretend being anxious to make some money and all three of them get into the same group. Then there came the time that they had put away at least fifty insurgents while the rest of them were sort of wondering what was accounting for all the deaths they were ordered to pull up stakes and catch the boats back to the states. They'd give it a window of sixty days and then send in another part of their organization.

This went on for a year and a half. Their score card was miraculous. In all that time they only lost three Marines. They also had another impact. The insurgents were starting to have difficulty recruiting others outside of the Marines. They were being turned down when the approached their fellow natives. No one had any idea of how their fellow insurgents had gotten their necks broken and for most part the knives were not left behind. So many men with gaping wounds in their backs. They were so troubled they were getting into arguments with each other. They couldn't hang the killings on anyone because they went back to their hideout after all their knifing.

Chapter

One Hundred Two

Inside their bunker they are merry. They have done a lot of damage. One of their greatest advantages was that they were giving the insurgents a bad rap. They were causing the rag heads to have a lack of recruits. That night they were drinking a great deal while they were saying a temporary goodbye to twelve fellow Marines. The ones left behind were going after another banquet of killings. Their bunker was so well camouflaged and fortified by their Seabees it could stay like that for a very long time. As they drifted from one store to another store buying things, putting up a front, they heard whispers between the natives that the insurgents were a very unhappy lot. This was fodder for a great deal of laughter at their base.

There was a light signal at three a.m. down by the shore as to the approaching boats. There were two boats with six men to a boat plus the motorman. As their boats went out they felt very proud of their accomplishments. They would sing a couple of choruses of the Marine hymn.

CHAPTER
ONE HUNDRED THREE

At the local naval detachment Rachel was holding her firstborn, a beautiful son built like his dad. Bruce and she were looking at him and smiling. The nurse came in and advised she had to put him back into the nursery.

"What are we going to name him?"

Bruce said "I'd like to name him what we call a nickname. No one uses their real name. Mostly nicknames are used."

"Well I don't know about that," said Rachel.

"O.k. we'll just call him Mike. Not Michael, but Mike."

"So Mike it shall be. That was easy. He'll be presidential material. My son the president. The 60th president of the United States."

"I've taken two weeks' leave and I'm even thinking of leaving the service."

"That would be fine with me. They did me a favor wanting me out. It was a blessing in disguise. I now have 150 franchisees and am making a fortune in profits. I'm now worth about $60,000,000. My sidekick is coming aboard in two months. He's taking care of the franchisees going forward. Our local business now has three techs and your brother when he feels like it. I'm thinking of franchising a new service."

"Bruce, don't talk business now. I'm expecting my parents in another hour."

"That's about the time my parents are due."

"My mother rang your parents up earlier today so that they could meet here. They're going out to dinner and talk about Mike for the whole evening. My father will also have him running for president. I'll be calling the captain down at Annapolis. I know he'll be up. I'm getting out of here two days hence. You know I was very curious about my campaigner. You know, the lieutenant I had with me. I found out he left Afghanistan quite some time ago. They wouldn't tell me where he went. It was classified, they said. That's really a mystery."

CHAPTER

ONE HUNDRED FOUR

Captain Cooper was with Colonel Windjammer over at the officer's club having lunch together. "Lunch is on me, Captain. It's not a casual lunch."

"Uh-oh. What's up?"

"You're doing a wonderful job with your men and you're not being properly compensated. You already have a history of an early promotion to captain. So I'm continuing by giving you one for major. That's right. You really have a special operation going here. It's the job of at least a major. So I suggest after we leave here you pick up some chevrons. I'm giving you your golden clovers and you can get the rest of them. I don't know if you realize it or not. You have generated talk about my battalion being a bad-ass outfit. That has given me spring in my step. You came up with the concept of suntanning your Marines, having them grow beards prior to assignment and came up with the idea of using the Seabees for their fortification. You have great vision. It's just amazing about your 180 degree turn around from being a student at Annapolis. I'm having it removed. At this point in your career it's ridiculous for you to have to put up with such drivel."

"You're getting a new commander pretty soon. I'm transferring to the Pentagon. I'll make it my business to keep in touch with you."

"You're running away on me?"

"Not my idea, Cooper. From what I hear no one really wants to work there that wears the uniform. They say it's a drab place, of course, except for the new spot, from the attack on 9/11."

CHAPTER

ONE HUNDRED FIVE

Kelly and Josh are down at the Jersey shore. She is having a great time with her new Glenn Miller. Josh has been writing some songs that have turned out to be quite popular among his musicians.

"Kelly, what attracted you to me, anyhow?"

"Josh you're the ultimate professional. Your stature in leading your organization. The sweet sound you put together. My love for music while teaching it. I guess maybe your looks had something to do with it." Now she was busting him. "How about you to me?"

"Are you kidding?! I'm listening to the perfection of my music. The instrumentation I have put together that created the sound I was looking for. Then I looked up to see how the people were receiving my work and you're staring right at me. It's not every day a guy has a beautiful woman such as yourself giving him such a penetrating look. You made me lose my concentration. I thought to myself 'wow what a looker'. You have to know that. Tell me, how many guys have you turned down that asked you for a date?"

"Just listen to you. You are funny. I have to admit it. I've been on the stuffy side. To be honest, sometimes I just feel conceited. It's not my fault. You know attractive women just keep getting stared at all the time. I've only turned down several guys."

"Only several?"

"O.k. I'd say four guys."

"Were you using good psychology turning them down?"

"I lied about having a guy. You don't hurt anyone's feeling that way. The psychology is someone else got to me first. They would reply something like 'lucky guy' and I'd say thank you."

"Kelly, a little white lie like that is really good psychology. The guy doesn't have to feel rejected that way."

"Well, if you're wondering about a romance with a guy you may land up getting engaged. If anything developed between us you'd be on hold for quite some time."

"Listen to Glen Miller. I'm already 35."

"Well, if it's children you're speaking of maybe you should have thought about that when being asked out! Your clock is running out!"

"A woman doesn't marry a guy just because her clock is running out. That would be cruel to anyone. She has to love him and desire him. It also wouldn't be fair to her kids either."

"Well I can't argue with that. Are you attracted to me in a what you might call serious way? Or am I just a handsome guy you like to spend some time with?"

Kelly gave him a look that could make his hair stand up with spikes. He didn't know if she was going to hit him or say something nasty.

"I take things one step at a time. We're at the beach today because we are attracted to each other. Who knows where that can take us?" She starts to laugh in an hysterical fashion and says, "I know what are parents are thinking, though."

"You don't have to go there. All they can see is grandchildren. Well, my sister came through for them several days back. I now have a nephew that I have to get interested in music."

"When am I going to get a chance to see him?"

"It will have to be when she visits my mom. This baby is going to crowd them out of where they're living now. My sister has great digs but that's just for her naval duties. I don't think she can have her family reside there. They're going to have to look for more expensive real estate. Bruce has been very successful and they can afford a nice house. But I think they'll have to go to Jersey for that.

"Kelly would you like to be going with me for a while?"

"What's that supposed to mean?"

"I thought you would know. We keep company for a year or so. What do you think about that?"

"I would like to be with you and attend affairs like a birthday for your nephew and share things with you beyond just a date."

"I'd like that a great deal. It would make my band guys jealous. Do you happen to have a decent singing voice?"

"If you're asking me would I consider singing with your group you'd be in for a big surprise."

"You mean you really can't sing that well, right?"

"Wrong. I've got a great singing voice. I've just never done anything about it. Mom and Dad have pushed me about that a few times."

"Really!"

"Very really. If I made up my mind to get involved several of those divas would have to move over!"

"Gee, you have me all excited."

"I could easily make a recording."

"What do you say you make one with the orchestra?!"

"I say let's do it."

"Kelly, this may turn into something ultra beautiful. You have no idea how hard my heart is pounding. Let's shorten that time from one year of seeing each other to a mere eight months. Then maybe, who knows, a possible engagement ring. What do you say?"

"I say that's the way. If I knew how that would affect you I would have told you I could sing earlier." That statement created a great deal of laughter. People sitting very close to them were slightly on the nosy side seeing that they were such a handsome couple. They seemed to smile when the laughter broke out.

"Tonight we are going to a fancy restaurant and have a very expensive dinner. I want to celebrate my featured new singer. I'm thinking I might ask for more money. Hey, if you're going to sing you should be paid for it. If you're as good as I'm thinking you'll be we will be an item to be reckoned with. The Josh Ferris orchestra with his new diva, Kelly--what's your surname, Kelly?" asked Josh.

"It's Scarpone. Kelly Scarpone."

"The Josh Ferris Orchestra with the beautiful Kelly Scarpone."

Chapter

One Hundred Six

Rachel had Mike on the bathenet as Bruce entered the apartment. He had a great big smile on his face. He went over to the bath and kissed his little one on the nose and his big one on the mouth.

"Kelly, I was with a realtor today and I have a house we'll look at tomorrow. I have the means to make the purchase, especially since real estate prices have come down so much. It's going for $350,000 and has four bedrooms and two baths, a living and dining room with a very large kitchen. The only thing I'm concerned about is the Navy transferring you to a new assignment."

"Well, the Navy is losing its luster to me. I'm not going to worry about a transfer. If that should have to come along I'll just retire from the Navy and join your business or start one of my own."

"My, that's great thinking. By that time you may make commander."

"I've got nearly thirteen years. I'll probably not be pensioned. I can't stay on this job for thirteen more years. They'll want a fresh commander. Unless they transferred me to the Pentagon, where officers don't want to be. For sure I'd leave."

Rachel was at the office with Mike. She was going over records of promotions and efficiencies. She started talking to Mike as he ga-gaged back to her. His teething had him in a state of deep slobbering. "Mike, you're making such a mess. I'll be feeding you lunch in about an hour." Her phone rang and she very lazily answered it. "Commander Ferris speaking, Major Cooper calling. What! Major Cooper. You've got to be kidding me. When did that happen? Just recently. How did it happen? My battalion commander is extremely impressed with me. He also expunged my record for my midshipman's days. I've been a very busy boy in training commandos. Are you free to visit? That's why I called. Can I take you to lunch? No. I now have a child. I don't think he'll get mad at me for taking you to lunch. What I mean is I'm feeding him lunch here in the office and I would gladly make it a three person lunch after I'm done with him. Want to come here for lunch? I can be there is twenty minutes. You're on commander.

Chapter

One Hundred Seven

As she opened the door to her campaigner she looked at him and said, "A newly-minted major."

"At your service."

"How I wish that could be. You have no idea how much I have missed you. You did so well for me."

"I'd gladly do it all over again."

"But you're a major now."

"Doesn't mean a thing to me. If I could help you I'd do it quick time. I'm going to tell you something since we're now the same rank. You'll be angry with me but I want to tell you anyhow."

"I'll try not to be angry with you."

"You're a very beautiful woman and I couldn't help but have feeling for you. I fell slightly in love with you back then."

Rachel broke into a laughing hysteria. The major felt almost slighted. However, she told him she had a confession to make.

"Well, since we're handing out compliments I've got one for you. You're a very handsome guy. I wasn't even engaged when you campaigned for me. You did a slight job on my emotions as well. However, I had to watch myself. For the time being I was your commanding office and any romance would have been a criminal act on our behalf. I actually wondered what a kiss would feel like from you then."

"I'm stunned. I can't believe it. We shared a romantic emotion."

"No we didn't share it. We thought it. Big difference."

"Does your husband know how fortunate he is with such a beautiful wife?"

"He does. Let's not speak of it anymore, please. I'll be feeling guilty. Do you like roast?"

"I sure do."

"Well you're in luck. I brought some with me for lunch. We'll enjoy after I feed my little rascal.

"So, what is it you've doing to merit this upward movement?"

"It's really classified. The only way I can tell you is in a simple way. My men have been doing a lot of killing. We're doing it to our advantage. To put it simply, they've been training to be cut throats and I mean that literally. We surprised the turban guys in Afghanistan, I'll tell you that much. One of my guys was so good at it he temporarily had a detachment he was commanding. He also earned himself a promotion to Gunnery Sergeant."

"Cooper, I am so impressed with you. I'll put in for another campaign and I think I'll get it. I had a grouch for a boss and he was transferred out. My new boss is higher in rank. He is a captain. I think I can sell him on the idea."

"That would be great. I'm sort of a free agent with what I have been doing. I can leave my second in command to take responsibility of the organization and take a temporary duty classification for a month. How does that sound?"

"That sounds great. On my past assignment, at Annapolis, I had a lieutenant junior grade working for me. A very attractive blond; she's coming up for a visit. Would you like to meet her? The problem is you'll probably fall in love with her. She is that hot. She's never met anyone she would like to hook up with her. What do you say to a blind date?"

"I'd feel more comfortable as just your dinner guest. A man with my responsibilities is not suitable for any romance."

"Now you're talking crazy."

CHAPTER

ONE HUNDRED EIGHT

The Prescotts are down at the real estate office and are in conference with the lady about the property he advised Rachel about.

"O.k. Mr. Prescott and Commander Prescott. We are going over to 975 Devine Lane. As I told your husband it is selling for $325,000. If you can appreciate the house, considering your husband's income level, it can be yours in a matter of sixty days."

As they came onto Devine Lane they wondered why it took the name of being a lane with such a high number. Rachel was in awe of the neighborhood. She heard gurgling coming from the back of the car with Mike making a mess out of himself.

"Boy Mike's a piece of work with his teething. I'm hoping I don't stand a chance of getting a sting while I'm nursing him."

"I'll never sting you while I'm nursing on you. She's parking the car. That's the house."

Rachel's expression was in a state of awe. She looked back to Bruce, back to the house and back to Bruce again. Her smile couldn't get any wider. "Bruce, I love the outside. I hope to love the inside just as much. It is beautiful. Well, the lady is waiting on us."

They alighted from the car and walked on over to the real estate agent.

"You're going to love this house. When I first listed it I began to think about buying it for my family. However, I didn't want to start a mortgage all over again."

They approached the front door and she worked the lock open. There was a very little hallway as they entered. Moving into a small vestibule the builder managed a spiral stair case to give the vestibule some depth. Rachel and Bruce both had their mouths open while Mike had his hand in his mouth.

"Well, let's go up stairs," said the agent. The master bedroom was very large with walk-in closets. The other three bedrooms were also a good size. They were about ten square feet less than the master. The closets were very large without being walk-in. Returning downstairs they went to living room where there was a beautiful fireplace and mantel. There was also a sizeable dining area.

"We've seen enough," said Bruce. "Sign us up for it. How could she not want it?!"

"I'll need a deposit of 20%. So that will come to $65,000 and a loan of $260,000 over a period of thirty years."

"No, I'm going to go for 25 years and if things go as well as they are I may go down to 20 years."

"If you do that you're going to get a penalty, you know that, don't you?"

"How much of a penalty would that be?"

"I'd say somewhere around $3,000."

"I'll live with it."

"Give my husband a little success and he would possibly get together with the big boys. He seems to forget at this particular time he's a little guy."

"Well, Mrs. Prescott, he strikes me as on his way to join the big guys, as you put it."

CHAPTER
ONE HUNDRED NINE

Rachel told Mom she was going to look for a house. Mom and Dad were conversing in the kitchen where Dad was drinking coffee and eating one of Mom's delights.

"Josh is coming over for dinner, Daddy."

"Mother, how many roasts do you make to keep Josh coming for dinner? He does eat out a lot. The food bill gets to be indigestible."

"It only seems like a lot. He's also here for spaghetti and other meals."

"Oh, I didn't realize it."

"I don't see you having a problem putting down a roast."

"Uh, now she's going to start picking on me. I can't talk about my own son without her having a kitten."

"There is no reason at all for picking on your son. He's going to bring fame to your name."

"How poetic!"

Now they see headlights coming into the drive way.

"That must be Josh. Bruce and Rachel park in the front with the baby. I'm going to tell them to park in the driveway and let Josh park in the front."

Josh opens the kitchen door and says, "Hi Mom, hi Dad. How are you guys?"

"We're waiting for Rachel to come over. She went to see a house today."

"Oh, that's wonderful. I didn't know that."

"Well, you're a busy person, Josh. And, you're turning out to be a promising business man. So, you and Kelly were at the shore. How was it down there?"

"My Kelly is going to sing with the band."

"Daddy, did you hear what he said?"

"I'm not deaf, Mother. I heard him."

"Daddy, it's not the fact that he said Kelly is going to sing with the band. He said my Kelly is going to sing with the band."

"Gee, Mom. You don't have to make a big deal of that. It was just an expression."

"Oh sure. It was just an expression."

"You have a grandchild now. Let me breathe, will you?"

"Well two grandchildren is better than one."

"Mom, why do you have to nag? When the Lord picks a wife for me I'll get married."

"You may not realize it, Josh Ferris, but you have a twinkle in your eye when you speak about Kelly. I'll bet her parents see a twinkle in her eyes."

"Not to change the subject, Mom, but that roast is causing me to float."

"When doesn't it cause you to float? You've been floating over roasts since you were five years old."

Bruce approaches the front of the house and parks with a great amount of excitement.

"Honey, I can't wait to tell Mom. I'm ready to explode."

"Don't do it here, Rachel. I need the car."

The front door starts to open and Mom yells, "Rachel, I heard the car. We're in the kitchen."

"Well, go into the living room, Mom. I want to change Mike. He was stinking us out of the car."

"Don't you talk about my grandchild that way. He can stink up the house all he wants. He's at granny's house now.

It's his right to stink it up."

"Brother, listen to her, Bruce."

"You might not know it, Mike, but granny has made royalty out of you." Mike is kicking his feet and gurgling.

They have now settled and hugged each other. "Rachel, don't hold out. What happened already?"

"Bruce will go to the realtor tomorrow and place a deposit down. I don't know where he got all that money from; hoping he hasn't done anything wrong."

"I beg your pardon. It wasn't long ago I was an agent of the Federal Bureau of Investigation. That's not the background of a thief. At least I don't think it is. Before we met, love, I had done a lot of investing that survived the recession. I don't know how that happened but it did. The Lord has been very good to me in that respect."

"Oh, you never told me about any investments that you made."

"We weren't involved at the time. It was none of your concern."

"Are you guys going to tell us about the house or are you going to go on about money before you met each other?"

"Mom, the house is beautiful. I can't wait for you to see it. I could not want anything more. My husband is not with the FBI anymore but he hasn't lost any of his sharpness."

"Well thanks for that," said Bruce."

"See, you guys can get along nicely. You had me worried there for a minute."

Dad was now starting to roll his eyes around. "One, two, three, would you stop yapping already. The house, the house. I want to hear about the house."

"Dad, you'll fall in love with the fire place. Something tells me you'll be there big time when we have you over for supper."

"So, would a week be enough time before you have us over for supper?"

"I'm afraid you'll have to give us about a month."

"Rachel, I'm going to hold you to that. Will you have a roast?"

"For you, Dad, I will have a roast."

"That will make me a very happy man. Thank you."

After all the explaining in detail, Mom said she wanted to help. Rachel replied that taking care of Mike would be a great help. So, Grandma was going to major in babysitting Mike. Josh took it all in and just hung around listening.

Bruce approached Josh and shook hands and started talking with him.

"Have you dated that lovely Kelly?"

"You might say that. We went to the Jersey shore on the weekend and had ourselves a great time. She advised me that she also sings but never wanted to be a singer. Would you believe she told me she could make a couple of the divas make room for her?"

"Well this is some revelation, Josh. Is that going to mean something to you?"

"She's going to sing with my group. I'll increase my fee, if I can get away with it, and pay her. Of course, I haven't heard her yet. But I take her word for it."

Just then the phone rang and Mom picked it up. She briefly spoke and looked at Josh and advised it was his call. "Hello Kel, didn't expect to hear from you. How's it going?" Bruce motioned Josh to come over to him. "Yeah," said Josh to Bruce.

"You have a speaker phone, right?" Josh nodded.

"Bruce is asking me something, Kel."

"Ask her to sing something so that we all can listen to her."

"It might not sound too good over the phone."

"Ask her anyhow."

"Kel."

"Yes."

"I'd like the family to hear you sing. We're all here. My sister is visiting because she just bought a new house."

"Good for her."

"Would you sing something?"

"Do you have any suggestions?"

"Well, this is going to come as a surprise to you. How about the Lord's Prayer instead of a popular song?"

"That's a great suggestion, Josh. I'd love to sing that.

"You let me know when everyone one is settled in their seats and are in a listening mode. I do not want anything but their absolute attention."

"Mom, Dad, Rachel, Kelly has advised me she is going to sing for us."

"She sings?"

"The stage is all yours." Everyone was very quiet. Mike wasn't even gurgling.

"Here goes. *OUR FATHER WHICH ART IN HEAVEN, HALLOWED BE THY NAME. THY KINGDOM COME, THY WILL BE DONE ON EARTH, AS IT IS IN HEAVEN.*

The surprise on every one's face had their mouths open. They couldn't believe how beautiful her voice was. They didn't make a peep.

GIVE US THIS DAY OUR DAILY BREAD AND FORGIVE US OUR SINS AS WE FORGIVE OTHERS. TO THINE BE THE GLORY AND THE POWER FOR EVER AND EVER AMEN."

"Kelly, you're not just whistling Dixie. We've have been mesmerized. What a secret you have been holding. I wasn't going to have the band get together for several days but now I'm calling them all in as soon as I can rent that hall. It may be available now. Would you come in and sing as soon as I can get it arranged?"

"Of course I can, Josh. So, you really appreciate my singing?"

"Let me put it this way. I'm sure glad I have met you."

"Watch out, Josh. You sound like you're getting romantic."

"What can I say? You sing like an angel and also look like one."

"Josh, that was so sweet of you."

"Kelly, I'll give you a call." Josh just looked at every one. He looked like he was in shock. His mother just stared at him.

"Josh, you're going to bring her into this family. Of course, you understand that, don't you?"

"Gosh Mom. Give me a breather. I don't want to rush into anything. I just met her. It's only been about five weeks. I don't know if we're really suited for each other."

"Josh, you're suited. You're suited. Believe me, you're suited."

"See Rachel. Now that you're married she's going to sit on me."

"I want grandchildren. I want grandchildren."

"Mike, Grandma is going to suffocate you."

His mother, looking up at the ceiling with a great deal of dignity, says, "I will not suffocate Mike. I will not suffocate Mike."

"Keep on telling yourself that. Sooner or later you're going to actually believe it."

All of a sudden everyone broke out in laughter.

"Josh, you're just as funny as Mom is. She has not returned to Earth since Mike was born."

Chapter

One Hundred Ten

Mike Smith was on the phone with headquarters. They were giving him a difficult time. They didn't like the performance of Bruce's replacement. Mike Smith was getting very frustrated with them. "What do you want me to do? You wanted Prescott out for some picayune reason and now you don't like his replacement. You have to give him some time. What did you say? If he doesn't improve in a six month period you want me to try and bring Prescott back in? Are you looney tunes? He's a businessman now in security. And he's successful at it. In fact, when I retire I'm going to go work with him. You're darn tootin. We have already discussed it.

"Don't you guys have anything better to do than to keep calling me up? I'm not getting insubordinate. I'm just stating facts. The director is on your back. Gee, you guys call me up again and I'm going to consider a transfer."

After hanging up he decides to call Bruce. The phone rings and rings and rings. He leaves a message. "Hi Bruce, it's Smitty. Would you get back to me? I want to talk with you. Thanks."

He calls Mike, Bruce's old sidekick. "Mike, it's Smitty. Let's lunch together. I'm buying. I want to talk to you." Mike is apprehensive since Smitty is his boss. "Anything wrong?"

"No. Nothing's wrong. I just want to talk to you about securities. See you in an hour."

Chapter

One Hundred Eleven

"Mom."

"That's my name. Don't wear it out."

"Kids are supposed to wear their mother out. I have something to tell you."

"Well, spit it out before I turn another birthday over."

"I sang the Lord's Prayer for Josh and his family on their speaker phone."

"Something wrong with you, Kelly? Maybe you should move back home, huh."

"I told Josh about my singing and he wants me to sing with the group."

Mom was staring at her. Then she placed her hands on her hips. Then she sat down.

"You want to say that again?"

"I had called Josh last night and he requested that I sing on the phone for his family. They loved it. He's in the throes of getting his men together and having me sing with the band."

"Oh, Kelly. That's wonderful. Your father will be happy to hear that. So, is he going to be calling me Mom?"

"It's been a very short time. We don't really know each other."

"What's to know? He's educated, handsome and talented. You're beautiful, educated and can sing and sing with style. You make a great looking pair. What's to know? Your father and I didn't act half as particular. Your father flipped when he met me. I wasn't about to waste a handsome man on anyone else. We played the dating scene for six months and got married. You have to make a science out of it."

"I'm not making a science out of anything. I just never met anyone that stirred me."

"Well, you have now. Right?"

"I guess you can say that."

"You're in your mid-thirties. Marry him. I wouldn't mind kissing him myself."

"Mom!"

"He's handsome, Kelly."

"Geez. Between you and him we'll have trophy grandchildren."

"I'm sure we will. That's two powerful sets of genes coming together. I don't believe I said that."

Kelly's cell phone burped and she looked at the name. It was Josh calling her. She turned on the phone and said hi. "Kelly, we're rolling tomorrow night. Come to Broadway Rentals on 45th and Broadway. Don't forget to bring your singing voice with you. I have to get music for a singer for these songs. We're going to go for four songs. We're bringing some good numbers. In fact I don't know if you even heard of them. One is titled 'Rocket of Love.' I did hear that song once. I was about ten years old. I remember, as a kid, liking that song. Another one is going to be a song that made Jack Martin sound great, 'Return My Love.' Then we'll do 'Danielle Honey' and lastly 'See the Pyramids." Then a couple of weeks later we'll break in today's numbers."

Kelly's mother signaled that she would like to speak to Josh. "My mom wants to speak with you."

"She does? Put her on."

"I just wanted to say hello, Josh. It's wonderful that she is going to sing with your group. I'm very happy about it." "That makes all three of us, Mrs. Sorenson."

"She bowled me over when she told me that."

"She told you about singing to my family on the phone?"

"Yes, she did."

"Tomorrow night we go with our initial singing practice."

"Take care, Josh."

"You too, Mrs. Sorenson."

Kelly took the cell phone back and advised Josh she had returned to the phone. "My mother had to horn in on my call. Yes, she took me by surprise. Until tomorrow, take care. I'm going to tell my classes tomorrow. They'll be in an uproar."

Chapter
One Hundred Twelve

There was a company formation with Cooper advising his detachment he was going on a recruiting campaign. He also introduced a new unit commander. "Men, we have a new commander. Colonel Windjammer was transferred out to the Pentagon. He has been replaced by Colonel John Tilly. He wants to say hello and get to know the unit a little."

They snapped to attention. He said, "At ease. I won't take but a couple of minutes of your time. Colonel Windjammer and I went to Annapolis together. He advised me that he was fortunate to have been in command of your detachment. He advised me that he did not want to interfere in your work; that he just came down to watch once in a while. He is very proud to have had you in his line of command. I'm going to follow him up just visiting, as well. I was told that you guys are bad. Sneaky bad and the best of the best. I know one thing I'm going to learn off of you. I was advised that you're the talk of the division. Your service to your country has been deemed glorious. Well, I'm glad to be here. Major Cooper will take over now." Without being commanded they stood at attention again.

"Well, I'll see you Marines in a month's time."

When Cooper got back into his office his clerk advised him he had a fax. The clerk said, "It's from a captain at a basic training outfit."

"You can do better than that," said Cooper.

"It's from Parris Island, sir."

"Let me see that."

To Major Cooper – Special Detachment of Advanced Skills.

I'm sorry to have held up your gunny and we talked about it. He wants to join your operation. Truthfully, I'm going to miss him. This will be a first for me. They don't come any better than him. He should be arriving at your unit tomorrow at 1500 hours.

Your organization has a reputation of being a killer unit and he can't get back to you any too soon.

"Gunny isn't going to stay a gunny. He is going to get a commission and be called Second Lieutenant. By golly, his surname fades when I need it. I'll need him big time because I have several men leaving. One transfer, one retirement and one's enlistment is over and he doesn't want to reenlist. I'll send a fax to Personnel in Washington, D.C. and advise them I need a corporal, sergeant and a private first class. Every time you think you are settled you're going to need new troops."

Chapter

One Hundred Thirteen

Mike and Smith were at lunch. Mike was nervous. He didn't like eating with the boss.

"Relax, Mike. We're on our own time. I placed a call to Bruce today but had to leave a message. How long are you going to stay with the Bureau? I'm just curious because we're both going to go in the same direction."

"You're coming aboard too?"

"Surprised, huh? Now, what I'm going to tell you is confidential. Don't let it get out."

"You have my word on that."

"I'm staying with the Bureau two more years, tops. Maybe even a lot less. Sometimes I wonder if the guys in D.C. have anything to do with themselves."

"They're on your case?"

"Yes. If it isn't one thing it's another. How are you doing with your new job as a part-timer with Bruce?"

"Smith, we're headed for success. His franchisees think he has a magic formula because of his Bureau background. I'm his executive vice president. I was handling all the calls that came in after work while he was on his honeymoon. What is it he is going to bring you on to do?"

"I think he'll want me to relocate and work another area of the country. He advised he'd bring me on as a vice president, too. When it happens, if it happens, I'll strut my stuff as a former Special Agent. Well, what are you going to have for lunch?"

"A bowl of clam chowder and a steak sandwich."

"That sounds great to me. I'll have the same."

Chapter

One Hundred Fourteen

As Rachel sits in her office and looks at a magazine her phone rings.

"Ferris here. Major, how are you? I just picked up a rental. You don't need one, you know. Well Commander, I'm not one for the subway. Major, would you like to just use our first names when we're not with the troops. That's okay by me. I'll be seeing you inside of a half hour. I'd like to take you to a couple of offices and advise the recruiters we're going to have another campaign. I'm very happy for several things, at this time. One is it will be great working with you again and the other is we just bought a house. I can't get more excited than I am. My former staff member, the one I told you about, is coming to visit in several hours. I told her about you. She said she'd be delighted to meet you. Tomorrow night I'll have the two of you over for supper. Then you can meet my husband and Mike, the newest member of the family. Commander, you're enriching my life."

Chapter

One Hundred Fifteen

The group was set up and ready to play. They all had a copy of the songs. First up was 'Wheel of Fortune.' It was the kind of song that she could enrich those high notes the way singers today never let go of the note and make it fancy. "What a looker," one of the guys whispered.

"O.k. Kelly. How do you feel about the song?"

"It's a piece of cake. I'm ready."

Josh put up his baton and "A one and a two." The music was now in the air. Kelly whipped out the bars and her face just lit up with *Return to Me.* There were nods of approval. The ones without their mouth on a mouthpiece were smiling very broadly. *Hurry home, hurry home, to my love and my heart.* That was it. Josh was thinking there was no doubt there would be a recording. All of a sudden he felt like he wanted her to be his. It came right out of the music. He realized he wanted to marry her. He was ready to set a date. He didn't care how long he had known her. He was in love. And she sang and sang and it was sssooooo gggooooodd.

They were on their way to her place and she asked if he wanted to come up for coffee.

"Oh, I could use a good cup of joe right now." They were sitting on the couch drinking and having a pastry.

"You know, you did something to me tonight."

"Yeah, so did you."

"What did I do?"

"I felt like you wrapped that music around me. It wasn't like I usually sing. I felt warmth coming from you. To be quite honest, without sounding conceited, I had the feeling you wanted me romantically. Like you wanted me." His mouth dropped open and he was speechless.

"Why are you looking at me that way, Josh? Are you thinking I'm weird?"

"Kelly, I was on the same wavelength. I felt just like you did. Out of nowhere I decided that I was in love with you. I told myself I wanted you." They very slowly went into an embrace, a kiss that they floated with. Then he whispered in her ear, "Will you marry me?"

Kelly looked at him in shock. She didn't know how to respond. They really had just met a short time ago. Maybe so but she knew she wanted him.

"Did you just ask me to marry you?"

"Yes," said Josh.

"You want me to marry you?" She held him a little tighter. "Josh I'll marry you. I wanted you weeks ago. Oh yes, I'll marry you. I'll marry you. You have no idea how much I love you. It just hit me the night I first saw you, a true case of love at first sight for me. That's why I made it my business for you to see me. And when you did I felt the electricity."

"Well, you walloped me big time. I mean I couldn't get back to being conscious of the band. I thought to myself, *What a lovely lady to put my arms around.*"

"Josh, my heart is beating so hard."

"Our hearts are beating together with one mighty big drum. Kelly, I'm so happy you stood in my line of sight. You are such a doll. A very beautiful woman. Would eight months from now be too soon to get married?"

"Are you kidding? I'd marry you tonight."

"As of now, doll, we are definitely engaged to be married. You will have an engagement ring within a week. I thought something was wrong with me. None of the attractive women I met flipped my switch."

"Tell me about it. Josh, I'm so happy. I'm not telling my mother yet. Not for at least a month. She'll never shut up." Josh started to laugh, almost in an hysterical way.

"That is a common problem. I'm following suit. My mom will never shut up, either. I have to think of my father, too. She'll give him one major headache. He'll need an apartment for a couple of days." Kelly broke out in a major laugh. "Kelly, I feel all shook up. I'm going home while I can still drive. I don't believe it. I'm getting married. I'm so glad I have some money put away."

"Josh, I've been putting money away for years. I've got over $100,000."

"That's great because it could go real fast. Good night. I'm on my way home."

Chapter

One Hundred Sixteen

Smith's phone rang and he picked it up quickly, hoping it was Bruce returning his call. "Hello. It's Bruce. I'm returning your call. I'm sorry it took me so long but it couldn't be helped. I don't believe how it's going. I would have never have believed it if someone would have told me." That's wonderful. What does this concern? Are you calling about that possible position I might have for you after you retire? I didn't take you long to figure that out. When do you figure on calling it quits? Not as long as I had thought. Are they aggravating you again? I shouldn't be discussing Bureau business with you. I can't go into it; however, yes, they are aggravating me again. How much time you have in? Twenty-five years. See, one thing good about my job offers is they don't have to be big bucks. You have your pension to beef up your income. What would you think about starting an office in Los Angeles? Why Los Angeles? The Hollywood crowd and their fantastic estates. Show biz people are good potential customers. They'd get the best of the best. Can you still handle it the way it is? I can; however, it's starting to get hectic. I just bought a house and I need to do some work. What do you say I come aboard is six months? What do you say to a starting salary of a mere $50,000? Well, like you said, that's on top of my pension. If it goes my way, Smith, I'll double it in 18 months. You'll be vice president of West Coast Operations. You don't mind if I talk about it with the wife, do you? Absolutely not. You need her blessings.

CHAPTER

ONE HUNDRED SEVENTEEN

It was Saturday night at the Italian restaurant of the Di Chaimos. This was the fourth Saturday and word was getting around. They had to set up some extra tables to accommodate more patrons. Now they had a problem. How long could they do it legally? If this was going to be a constant entertainment segment of their entertainment venue they were going to have to have to expand that room. Father and son were exuberant. Their food was the best and so was their entertainment. They had just been interviewed by the newspaper for dining and their write-up was a week away.

The orchestra was already a famous part of the restaurant. They were even attempting to come up with a venue name. They were thinking Di Chiamos & Orchestra Ferris.

"Are you nervous, Kelly?"

"Not on your life. I not only have my family here; we also have friends and neighbors. That's one reason the room is flooded with humanity."

"When do you want to sing?"

"I'll sing on the fifth number," said Kelly

"The fifth number it is. 'Wheel of My Heart.'"

I secretly told my dad about us. What a smile he had on his face. He said to me, 'that gorgeous girl of yours is going to be my daughter-in-law? Josh, you have made your old man a happy man. I'll be surrounded by beauty. Hey, don't wait a lifetime to have kids.'"

Kelly burst out laughing. She placed her hands on her face. "Josh, your dad is something else. He is going to be a lot of fun. I'm going to love him. He also happens to be a handsome man. You took looks from both of your parents. Life is going to turn out to be an adventure."

Josh got the attention of his musicians and got them playing. The roar of the crowd diminished and the music took over. The patrons were slowly coming onto the floor. What Josh was doing for this restaurant... Their business picked up by 35%. They were going to have to talk to their lawyer about when they definitely would have to expand.

Josh nodded to Kelly. She stood up and stood just a foot away from him. "Ladies and Gentleman, tonight I'm introducing a new feature into our entertainment group. Her name is Kelly Scarpone. She is a professor of music at a local university. She's going to sing 'Wheel of Fortune.' It will be very different from the style of the 1960s. I give you Kelly Scarpone." The roar of clapping was deafening.

The band lit into the melody and the music hardly resembled the earlier version with changing the value of the notes. Kelly could work those notes into such a pattern it was amazing. She could truly make the divas move over for her.

"Dad, listen to her sing," said Jim. "She is something else. I say he marries her. What do you say?"

"I say there is no question about it. It's just a matter of when. We'll have to do something real special for him. I don't know what but it will have to be special."

As the evening ended all the musicians told Kelly they hoped she was going to be a member of the orchestra.

CHAPTER

ONE HUNDRED EIGHTEEN

Josh met with the two proprietors of Di Chiamos. He had to get Kelly aboard for a paycheck too. She wasn't part of a charity. He knocked on the office door. He heard the voice tell him to come in.

"Josh, things are unbelievably fantastic. If you're here to bargain for Kelly, I'm all ears. How much do you want for her singing? Kelly, you are absolutely great. I wish you would go into recording," said the older Jim.

"She is, Jimmy. Before the end of the month we'll make an album of about ten numbers."

"Well thank you, Josh. Jimmy, I just learned about it just like you did. We're going to record, Josh? And he didn't even ask me if I wanted to. Did you?"

"No, I didn't; however, I certainly didn't think you would mind. Jimmy, would you consider $200 for a gig and if she does well with a record we'll have to go for a thousand on increments. Something like $50 dollars more a week on a monthly basis."

"You missed law school, Josh. That is very equitable. She'll probably leave us if she should hit it big. I mean there would be no point in her bothering anymore. But until such a time we'll go great guns with her."

Chapter

One Hundred Nineteen

Josh got home late and wondered why the lights were still on in the house. They never stay up this late. His mother and father had been waiting for him.

"Why are you guys still up?" His father just stared at the floor and his mother was cross with him. He could see that. "Mom, what are you sore about? You can't hide it and you aren't waiting up for nothing."

"What's with the secret, Josh? Your father gave you away this evening. What, you tell him and don't tell me? You want to deny me the joy of knowing that beautiful woman is going to be my daughter-in-law? This woman with such a terrific voice––you should be ashamed of yourself. I'm your mother and have a right to know."

"I'm sorry, Josh. It just slipped out of my mouth and I had to explain. You know your mother is tough."

Dad almost didn't want to lift his head. He felt bad about letting his son down and having his wife condemn Josh to death.

"It's o.k. Dad. I'm not going to hold it against you. So Mom, are you going to be angry with me for a while?"

"No! I'm not going to be angry with you for a while. I got it off my chest. Everything is o.k. now."

Mom jumped out of her seat and wrapped her arms around Josh and said into his chest, "I'm so happy, Josh. You have no idea what joy this brings me.

"Please don't nag me about grandchildren," said Josh "You'll probably end up with three of them. That'll keep you busy and spending your social security money on them and on top of all that, they're going to be knock-out children wanted by the movie world and fantastic singers and instrumentalists."

"Josh, after all that you said I'll take that to bed with me," said Mom.

"I heard every word of that, Josh, and I'm taking that to bed with me, too."

"I know I was the one to say it, but I'll take that to bed with me as well."

Chapter

One Hundred Twenty

Josh lay in bed thinking of his new fiancé. He really did not want to go to sleep. Well, she wasn't sleeping either. She was actually in shock. A splendid shock. She was hoping not to slip and mention it to her mother. The simplifier. What a catch she had. She figured she would in the next hundred years finally meet a guy. But such a handsome guy that all the gals are going to envy her for. The owner of an orchestra of fifteen pieces and her being what they want, really want. This is not Heaven, but only a mile short of it.

In Reverence

War is the worst thing to happen to life. What is worse than war is to be killed and go from one Hell to another Hell. Have you ever thought of that? Now, take note of what I'm going to say about this.

Just because there are numerous religions in the world that does not mean God is open to welcoming all believers. It does not work that way. So, what does he look for in a sea of recognitions? Let's look at this a good deal longer. A great many people consider themselves to be very good in character. They give money to good causes and hope that God is pleased. They want to be in good standing with their creator.

However, they don't think the way he does. Jesus volunteered before there was any form of humanity to get involved with.

A great many people have no idea that Jesus loves his father so deeply and all he wants to do is be obedient and loving for his father He needed to be the sacrifice because no one else had what was needed to give to God himself. Because he was the only one without sin, he had to sacrifice himself being so that people could recognize the need to have a savior and fill the populace through the blood of Christ and are welcomed into eternity.

Printed in the United States
By Bookmasters